The gu

His eyes were wide with a mix of anger and disbelief that his team had been taken down so swiftly.

Bolan hit him with a savage volley that cut the man down like straw in the wind, dumping his tattered and bleeding body on the ground.

The last echo of autofire drifted off into the trees. Wind rattled the brittle foliage, dislodging hard crusts of snow from the branches. Bolan's boots crunched over the ground layer as he moved from man to man, checking for signs of life and moving weapons clear. He had counted his targets and they were all down.

The Executioner's shots had been delivered with total accuracy.

MACK BOLAN ®

The Executioner

The Don Pendleton's Executioner®

DEADLY CONTACT

A GOLD EAGLE BOOK FROM

WORLDWIDE®

TORONTO • NEW YORK • LONDON
AMSTERDAM • PARIS • SYDNEY • HAMBURG
STOCKHOLM • ATHENS • TOKYO • MILAN
MADRID • WARSAW • BUDAPEST • AUCKLAND

First edition February 2007
ISBN-13: 978-0-373-64339-4
ISBN-10:   0-373-64339-X

Special thanks and acknowledgment to
Mike Linaker for his contribution to this work.

DEADLY CONTACT

Printed in U.S.A.

Go into emptiness, strike voids, bypass what he
defends, hit him where he does not expect you.

—Ts'ao Ts'ao, 155–220 A.D.

When I plan a mission I make sure my enemies will
never know what hit them.

—Mack Bolan

THE
MACK BOLAN
LEGEND

Nothing less than a war could have fashioned the destiny of the man called Mack Bolan. Bolan earned the Executioner title in the jungle hell of Vietnam.

But this soldier also wore another name—Sergeant Mercy. He was so tagged because of the compassion he showed to wounded comrades-in-arms and Vietnamese civilians.

Mack Bolan's second tour of duty ended prematurely when he was given emergency leave to return home and bury his family, victims of the Mob. Then he declared a one-man war against the Mafia.

He confronted the Families head-on from coast to coast, and soon a hope of victory began to appear. But Bolan had broken society's every rule. That same society started gunning for this elusive warrior—to no avail.

So Bolan was offered amnesty to work within the system against terrorism. This time, as an employee of Uncle Sam, Bolan became Colonel John Phoenix. With a command center at Stony Man Farm in Virginia, he and his new allies—Able Team and Phoenix Force—waged relentless war on a new adversary: the KGB.

But when his one true love, April Rose, died at the hands of the Soviet terror machine, Bolan severed all ties with Establishment authority.

Now, after a lengthy lone-wolf struggle and much soul-searching, the Executioner has agreed to enter an "arm's-length" alliance with his government once more, reserving the right to pursue personal missions in his Everlasting War.

Prologue

Bosnia, 1995

The sharp light of morning was accompanied by a chill appropriate to the mood of the day. A fine mist rained over the wooded terrain, the cold drizzle building until it slipped from the green leaves of the trees. It dripped onto the bared heads of the tight group shuffling forward from the truck that had brought them to this place. Five men and a single woman. They walked with the heavy tread of individuals aware of their fate, unable to do anything to alter it, yet clinging to some vague hope there might be some last minute reprieve.

They were surrounded by a three-man armed escort—men clad in better clothing than their captives. While the six wore ordinary dress, the escorts were comfortable in weatherproof coats and hats. No one spoke. There was no point. Anything that had been worth saying was in the past. It was time for closure.

Within the group, only one of them allowed emotions to show. One of the men sobbed quietly, his head down so that his chin rested on his chest. His tears

ran down his face and merged with the rain-soaked
material of his shirt. His hands were thrust deep into
the pockets of the crumpled, stained jacket he wore.
Once that jacket had been an expensive item from his
wardrobe. Now it showed the effects of his prolonged
incarceration. It had a number of tears in the fine
material, and some of the dark stains were from his
own blood. He knew he was about to die. He wanted
it to be different, but the line that prevented that had
been crossed many days ago. He had chosen his side,
as had the others in the group, and it had been the
wrong side. He was about to pay the price for his
decision, which in his heart he still defended. He knew
the people controlling his destiny were evil. They were
men who saw personal aggrandizement as their right,
contrary to the responsibility they carried for the coun-
tries they served. A defiant resistance to those illegal
activities had been the catalyst for the action taking
place in this isolated landscape.

Someone rapped out a harsh command, and the
group was herded to a stop in a clearing in the wooded
terrain. A deep pit had been dug. The dark mounds of
extracted earth edged three sides of the pit, glistening
in the rain. Already a thin layer of water had pooled in
the bottom of the pit. The armed escorts lined up
behind the six, the one who had given the command
glancing to his right at a shadowy gathering of men
standing just within the tree line. One of these men
stepped forward, into the light. A big man, with a hard-
boned face wet with rain. He was bareheaded, his thick

black hair lay tight against his skull. He exhibited no remorse as he faced the six.

"This was not inevitable," he said. "You chose your own fate by refusing to join us."

The woman turned to look him in the eye. One side of her attractive face still bore the discoloration that was the result of a severe beating.

"Murderers always try to justify their crimes," she said. "You are no different. In the end you are all no more than backstreet scum, criminals and thieves, and one day your actions will reach out and drag you down into the grave with us." She spit in his direction. *"Do your worst, you bastards."*

A swift nod and the escorts raised the automatic weapons they were carrying. There was no preamble, no final words or comfort for the victims. The clearing echoed to the vicious crackle of autofire that riddled the six with 9 mm bullets. The writhing bodies tumbled forward into the pit, screaming out their final moments as they hit the rain-sodden earth. Torn flesh, shredded clothing, the final spurts of blood. A pink haze floated for seconds over the open pit, dissipating in the continuous rain.

"Fill it in," the big man said. "Then get out of here. Report to me in the morning."

He turned then, flicking a finger at the others standing with him and they merged with the dark trees, retracing the steps that had brought them to this place of slaughter. Minutes later they emerged from the trees and climbed into waiting SUVs. Powerful engines purred to life and the small convoy moved off, following the curve of the thin track, disappearing into the gray mist until there was no sign they had been there.

At the pit site, the escort squad had exchanged their weapons for long-handled shovels. They worked quickly, scooping the wet earth back into the pit, covering the bodies, then dragging clumps of shorn foliage and leaf mold over the plot. The rain would soon reduce their boot prints to nothing, washing away evidence of their activities, and it would not take long for the forest to reclaim its disturbed ground. The grass would grow, and the foliage would weave and tangle its way back.

AN HOUR LATER THE SITE WAS deserted. The distant rumble of the departing truck had long since faded, leaving only the sound of the rain to break the solitude.

From the far side of the clearing a dark figure emerged from concealment. He was a lean, tight-featured man clad from head to foot in camouflage clothing that had allowed him to remain unseen until he stepped into the open. Even his face was striped with camo paint, so his eyes stared out from the mask, bright and feral. He carried an expensive, professional camcorder in his hands. The equipment was state-of-the-art and was fitted with a powerful variable-focus lens arrangement that allowed for tight, detailed close-ups even from a distance. The man had been in place well before the events at the pit had taken place. He had recorded the whole episode, making certain that his tape logged every face, of victims as well as the killer escort. He had also focused in tightly on the group by the trees, recording their presence at the massacre. He stood and took a final pan of the area, ending by holding his camera on the camouflaged area of the burial site.

He had just completed his filming when he felt the soft vibration of his cell phone in his pocket. He unzipped the flap and took out the phone, pressing the button to open the connection.

"Are you finished?" the voice of his employer asked.

"I was about to leave."

"You have it?"

"Oh, yes. Everything. They are all identified. It is all on the tape."

"Excellent. You know what to do?"

"As we discussed. Give me until the end of the week and it will all be documented."

"I will talk to you then. Now I have to go. They are ready to start the proceedings. We have the past to toast and our assured futures to celebrate."

The cell phone went silent and the man put it away. First he placed the camera in the soft, waterproof case he had tucked inside his zipped jacket. He slung the case over his shoulder by its webbing strap, then turned and began his long tramp back through the forest to where he had left his car. He had at least a half hour walk ahead of him, but he consoled himself with the anticipation of the warm apartment waiting for him. He would do what he needed to do with the video cassette and the material he had recorded over the past few weeks. He also thought of the money it would bring him, courtesy of his *employer,* and the payments in the future that would ensure he continued to enjoy his life of upcoming luxury. During his walk back to his concealed car, he never once gave any thought to the six people he had seen slaughtered. In his mind they had ceased to exist the moment the fiery 9 mm bullets had ripped into their bodies.

Present Day

Throw a pebble in water, and the waves extend outward with a speed that reaches far beyond the moment of its creation.

For Mack Bolan those ripples had already reached out to engulf someone he knew and had drawn him to this isolated, derelict farm in upstate Virginia on a rescue mission about to go hot.

Armed and clad in blacksuit, he erupted out of the dark shadows and confronted the three-man crew holding Erika Dukas hostage. The crew had been waiting for their orders and were on less than full alert. They had been promised cash for their part in the operation. It had been good pay for a relatively easy job, and the men were congratulating themselves on the easy money.

They were unprepared for the tall, blacksuited Executioner as he opened the abandoned farmhouse door with a powerful kick from a booted foot. As the door flew open, sagging from one hinge, Bolan appeared and lashed out with his Uzi at the closest of the three men before him. The man tumbled back, blood welling from the heavy gash in his head, stumbling to the floor. Bolan turned his attention to the other two as they produced automatic pistols, the suppressed Uzi spitting fire as he squeezed the trigger, tracking the muzzle from left to right, then back again, kicking the stunned kidnappers off their feet. As the last of the 9 mm shell cases clinked to the floor Bolan strode across the room, laying his Uzi on the wooden table he passed and used his Ka-bar fighting knife to cut through the bindings securing Erika Dukas to a wooden chair.

She ripped the duct tape from across her mouth.

"Another one outside..." she gasped before drawing breath.

Bolan helped her to her feet.

"There was," he said quietly.

It was his only reference to the man who had been standing *guard* outside. He slid the knife back into its sheath, but not before Dukas caught a glimpse of the blood smear on the blade.

"Oh," she whispered.

Bolan's concern over Dukas drew his attention, momentarily, from the men he had taken out. If he had to come up with any excuse as to his momentary lapse in concentration, it would have referred to the clubbing he had received back at Tira Malivik's apartment. The slight concussion had not entirely cleared, and it had left him less than fully alert.

Behind him a bloody figure rose awkwardly from the floor, turning to make a grab for the Uzi on the table.

The woman's gasp of surprise warned Bolan.

He turned and powered himself across the room, his eye on the weapon too, aware of the end result if he failed to commandeer it. The kidnapper had less distance to cover and he moved fast, a near-triumphant smile on his bloody lips as he reached out for the submachine gun. His fingers closed over the metal, yanking the Uzi toward him. Bolan was still a couple of feet away. He made a last-ditch attempt, launching himself forward and across the table, sliding over the surface, and slammed bodily into the kidnapper.

The impact sent the guy stumbling back, almost losing his grip on the SMG. He crooked a finger around the trigger and hauled the muzzle around to track on Bolan. The Executioner kept his forward motion. He rolled across the far side of the table, landing on his feet and swinging out his right arm, delivering a smashing fist that clouted the man across the side of his face. He reached for his holstered Beretta.

The other man grunted, pain flaring. He swung the SMG in a vicious arc that cracked against Bolan's shoulder and followed it with a brutal kick that caught the soldier in the side, spinning him away from the table. The kidnapper pulled the muzzle of the SMG on line, increasing pressure on the trigger.

Bolan tried again for his holstered Beretta, aware he was competing with a man with his finger already on the trigger.

The sound of the single shot made Bolan stiffen, expecting the impact of a bullet hitting home. When it did, it wasn't Bolan who was the victim. He was looking directly at the kidnapper and saw the bloody exit hole that appeared in the man's left shoulder. The bullet had entered to the right of his spine, coring its way through his body and blowing clear, taking bone fragments and fleshy debris with it. The man didn't even have time to scream before he fell, letting go of the Uzi when he hit the floor.

Bolan scooped up the weapon, ran a quick check, then turned to the shooter.

It was Erika Dukas.

The Stony Man Farm translator was still on her knees where she had made a grab for the pistol dropped by one of the other kidnappers. She still held the weapon in both hands and stared in stunned silence at the man she had shot.

Bolan went straight to the woman, crouching in front of her. He gently pried the pistol from her trembling fingers, then placed a large and comforting hand on her cheek.

"We need to get clear of this place, Erika. Before others come."

She looked at him and he saw her eyes were threatening to spill over with tears.

"I...needed to stop him. He was going to kill you. Wasn't he going to kill you?"

"I'm a lucky guy to have you at my back. Now let's get out of here. We can talk this over when we're safe." He took hold of her arm and helped her to stand, conscious she had transferred her gaze to the sprawled body. "He can't hurt us now, Erika. Come on, we need to go." His voice was low and gentle, his words soothing the turmoil she was undoubtedly experiencing.

Dukas bent to pick up something from the floor. It was the fanny pack she had been wearing. She secured it around her waist.

"Time to move," Bolan said. "We need to talk."

"I'm surprised you have time for conversation," she said as she followed him outside and away from the silent house.

Bolan didn't reply. He led her back the way he'd come, a walk of at least a quarter mile through the rainy darkness before they came to the concealed Jeep Cherokee. Dukas slid onto the passenger's seat and waited while Bolan opened the tailgate door. He got out of his combat harness and pulled a lightweight black leather jacket over his blacksuit. He wore the 93-R in a shoulder rig under the jacket. When he joined Dukas, he handed her a 9 mm SIG-Sauer pistol and a clip-on hip holster he had taken from his duffel bag.

"From here you go armed. I know you've done some time on the firing range. I've heard you have a steady hand and a good eye," Bolan said.

"Paper targets don't shoot back," she said as she ejected the magazine, checked it, then clicked it back. "But I suppose I just proved I can handle a gun."

Bolan saw how capable she was with the pistol. Her movements were smooth and unhurried. He watched her ease the safety on before she put the gun away, adjusting the holster on her hip. He handed her a couple of extra magazines, and she dropped them in her pocket.

"These people we're dealing with don't appear to have much regard for life. We've already seen how they operate. If we meet up again and the need arises, just remember it's your choice. Your life, or theirs," Bolan stated.

She nodded. "I understand. I won't let you down."

As he drove Bolan checked out the still, silent figure beside him. He understood what she was going through, and though he kept his thoughts to himself he knew that Dukas would need to come to terms with what she had just done.

All the right reasons were not going to make the slightest difference. Justification, moral right, good versus bad, none of that would wipe away the cold, hard fact that Erika Dukas had taken a life. When the initial shock wore off, Bolan knew Dukas would ponder the stark facts and realize she had sent a man to a morgue slab. The full realization might knock her back and render her incapable of accepting what she had done. On the other hand her resolve might be strong enough to accept the facts and let her move on. For the moment he allowed her the privacy of her own thoughts.

They were still short of the main highway when Bolan picked up the flash of headlights in his rearview mirror. He watched them until he counted at least two vehicles in pursuit.

"*Company,*" he said.

Dukas twisted in her seat and studied the oncoming vehicles.

"You think they're coming after us?"

"Out here? Off-road? I don't imagine they're tourists. They must have arrived just after we left," Bolan replied.

He put his foot down, increasing the Cherokee's speed. The dirt track they were on did little to assist a smooth passage, and the fact the road was water-logged from the rain only added to the treacherous surface. The SUV managed the terrain, but the ride was uncomfortable.

"This is just crazy," Dukas shouted above the rising howl of the engine. *"What the hell are we doing out here?"*

Bolan kept his eyes on the road ahead, peering through the streaming windshield where the wipers were struggling to keep the glass clear. The twin head-light beams danced and shimmered in the downpour as Bolan fought the wheel. The Cherokee slid back and forth, brushing the drenched foliage on each side of the narrow strip. More than once Bolan felt solid thumps as the Cherokee's heavy tires hit some unseen object.

He concentrated on the road ahead, knowing that the difficult driving conditions would hamper their pursuers as much as it did them. It was a small conso-lation, but at least it was *something*.

A bend appeared, and Bolan worked the wheel and the gears to control the Cherokee. He felt the rear slide away and compensated, bringing the heavy SUV back on track. He felt the road start to slope. It wasn't a steep incline, but under the conditions it did little to help, except to increase their speed.

To the north thunder rumbled, a deep threatening sound that heralded the sudden crackle of lightning. The jagged fork lanced across the cloudy sky, briefly illuminating their surroundings and adding to the general din.

"What next?" Dukas asked. "Do they have tornadoes around here as well?"

The solid thump of bullets striking the Cherokee grabbed their attention. Bolan tried to erase the sound from his mind, but the increasing accuracy of the gunfire meant that sooner or later they would sustain a fatal hit. The tailgate window exploded as rising gunfire hit the glass, almost as a grim warning.

Bolan felt the trail dip suddenly. The front wheels twisted, the big vehicle swayed and then lurched off the trail, sliding down the steep slope. Bolan fought the drift, but despite his powerful grip he was unable to bring the SUV back under control. He felt the right side wheels leave the ground as the Cherokee started to tilt.

"Grab something," he yelled at Dukas.

The Cherokee rolled, and Bolan and Dukas were helpless as it commenced its bouncing, twisting descent. The last thing he was able to do was turn off the engine before the falling vehicle turned their world into a dizzying, wild ride that could have left them severely injured, or even dead, if they hadn't been securely strapped in. It didn't stop them from being jolted, suspended by safety harnesses, senses jarred and knocked out of kilter by the careering Cherokee. Sometime during the fall the windshield shattered, and sleet and mud entered the passenger compartment.

And then it ceased.

As swiftly as it had begun, the spinning, bruising tumble stopped. The vehicle lay on its left side. The creak of distorted metal and the sound of the wind penetrated their senses as they fought to push away the effects of the crash.

Bolan managed to hit the release button and free himself from his belt. He was on his side, pressed up against the driver's door. He ached, and the side of his head was bloody from where he had banged against the window. He blinked his eyes a few times to get them back in focus. His attention was drawn to something *above* him.

It was Dukas, still caught in the restricting safety harness. In the pale light he could see the frustrated expression on her face.

"I can't find the damn release," she said.

Bolan sat up and reached between the tilted seats. "Ready?"

He hit the button and Dukas slid from the harness and tumbled free. For a moment they were entangled, and in another place at another time Bolan might have enjoyed the contact. But their position left them vulnerable to attack, so any fleeting moment of closeness was abandoned instantly.

Dukas had the same thoughts and she hauled herself off him, ducking her head through the windshield gap, half falling as she pushed into the open, feeling her hands sink into the chill ooze of mud.

Bolan was close behind. He had spared a few seconds to search for the duffel bag holding his backup weapons, grabbing the handles and hauling the bag with him, then followed Dukas out of the Cherokee.

The cold rain hit him as he pushed to his feet, turning to see if his companion was safe. She was leaning against the vertical hood of the upturned Cherokee, checking the pistol he had given her earlier.

No need to remind her of the priorities, Bolan thought.

He took out the Beretta and made sure it was ready for use. He set it for single shots. He had two spare magazines for the weapon, plus the one already loaded. It would do. There wasn't time to break out anything else. He checked the long slope they had come down. Headlights broke up the gloom, and he saw the dark figures clustered around the pursuit vehicles. The light faded just as quickly, and in that brief moment Bolan made his decision.

"Highway is in that direction," he whispered. "We need to reach it if we can."

Dukas nodded. Her face was slick with rain, her dark hair soaked.

Bolan touched her arm and pointed her in the direction they needed to go.

The ground underfoot was waterlogged and spongy. The mud clung to their feet and slowed them. The constant fall of sleet drove in at them. Bolan let Dukas pull ahead a few feet so he was able to keep her in sight. Bringing up the rear, he checked their back trail and saw the bouncing shafts of light from the pursuit vehicles as they headed slowly down the slope. They halted beside the overturned Cherokee, and Bolan could imagine the anger and frustration the crews would experience when they found it empty. Once they realized their quarry was still up and running they would pick up the chase again.

Up ahead Dukas lost her footing and went down on her hands and knees. Bolan reached her side and stood over her. About to offer a free hand to help, he was waved aside as she stood upright.

"I'm fine. Thanks for the gesture." She pushed wet hair back from her mud-spattered face.

"Come on then," he said.

They cut off across the muddy landscape, Bolan aware that the pair of vehicles would catch up with them soon enough. He was looking out for anything that might offer cover if the need arose, but there didn't seem to be anything to break the unending stretch of relatively flat terrain.

The sudden crackle of autofire told them their pursuers were not waiting any longer. The shots were way off target.

"If those chase cars get in range, try for the tires. It should slow them. Put *them* on foot too," he said.

"Seems reasonable," Dukas answered without breaking her stride.

The first pursuit vehicle closed on them quickly and Bolan snapped out a single command.

"Down."

Dukas dropped, splaying her body across the muddy earth, propping herself on her elbows, the pistol in a two-handed grip. The Executioner was down himself in the same breath, dropping the duffel bag beside him, the 93-R tracking the driver's door.

The SUV was only yards from them, slowed almost to a stop as the occupants searched for their quarry.

"Did they see us?" Dukas asked above the hiss of the rain.

"Most likely didn't," Bolan answered. "Easy to miss us in these conditions."

"What do we do?"

"Use it to our advantage. Start cutting down the odds. You go for that front tire. *Now.*"

She didn't challenge his command, simply eased the muzzle of the SIG-Sauer around and stroked the trigger three times. The first shot missed. The next pair chunked into the tire, which blew with a soft sound. The SUV lurched to a stop.

Bolan hit the driver's window with a pair of close shots, the glass imploding and the wheelman jerking in his seat as the 9 mm slugs hit home. Coming up on one knee Bolan triggered more shots at the SUV's windows.

Confusion stalled the passengers and by the time they had overcome it, two were dead, another wounded, and the rest frantically pushed open the doors on the opposite side of the vehicle, tumbling clear. High ground clearance left them exposed, and Bolan laid his fire into the crouching figures, seeing one go down before the others broke apart.

"The other car's coming," Dukas warned.

"I see it," Bolan said. "Start to back up, flat to the ground. And keep going. Take the bag with you."

"What about—"

"Go."

His tone warned her not to resist. Dukas wriggled away from her position, sliding her body through the greasy mud, dragging the duffel bag behind her. She had gone only a few yards when the stutter of a sub-machine gun sounded. She felt the impact as the line of slugs churned the earth. She continued to crawl, surprisingly calm despite the entirely new experience of being under hostile fire. There was something almost unreal about the situation, but she didn't pause to question it. Later, if there *was* any later, she would.

Bolan had started to move in the opposite direction, working his way around to the rear of the stalled SUV. He was making his plan as he moved, aware of the ever-changing situation, using the confusion that had to have been present within the ranks of the opposition. They had been anticipating a run down of their quarry, not the opposite where the hunted became the hunter. Bolan's strike against them had made them stop and reconsider. If he kept that feeling alive by taking the fight to *them*, rather than simply running, he might yet gain full advantage. It was worth the risk. Bolan had never lost a fight through quitting, and his warrior mentality always urged him forward, using superior thought and tactics.

He slithered his way through the mud, low to the ground, and he noticed that the gunfire had ceased. The targets had vanished and the gun crew was evaluating what to do next. They were in open country, the terrain unforgiving and the driving rain simply adding to the difficulty of locating their quarry. That was their problem. As Bolan got closer he saw figures silhouetted against their vehicles, with headlights still blazing. The enemy stood out clearly. It suggested that these men were not seasoned fighters in this kind of situation. He figured they were probably a hired gun crew from an urban background.

Bolan drew himself against the bulk of the vehicle and hauled himself up on one knee. Peering around the edge, he counted the opposition. Three close to the second car, a fourth standing off a few yards, cradling a submachine gun as he peered into the misty gloom.

"No way we're going to find them out here," one of the men said.

"Billingham said that it we don't find 'em we don't need to go back."

Someone laughed nervously, then said, "What's he going to do? Wipe us all out?"

"Now I know you never worked for him before, because that's just what he will do."

Bolan snapped in a fresh magazine and cocked the Beretta. He rose to his full height and stepped out from behind the SUV, his finger easing the selector switch to 3-round bursts.

He took out the SMG man first, the 9 mm bullets catching the guy in the chest as he turned to rejoin his three partners. The 93-R's muzzle was already tracking in on the trio as the shot man went down. Bolan broke away from the SUV, moving in close as he triggered repeat bursts, the slugs ripping through clothing and into flesh, spinning his targets off their feet. They collided with one another as they toppled into the mud.

Bolan went directly to the SUV and opened the driver's door. He slid behind the wheel, fired up the engine and swung the vehicle around, moving in the direction Dukas had been crawling. He braked and stepped out of the SUV.

"Erika? Over here," he shouted.

In the beam of the lights he saw her mud-caked shape emerge from the mire, then haul herself toward him.

"Don't," she warned. "One crack and I'll lose it." She flicked mud from her face. "Can you believe women pay to have this stuff plastered over them to improve their looks?"

"In your case it looks like it's working already," Bolan said.

"Until I work that out I'll consider it a compliment," she said as she tramped by him. She yanked open the passenger door and dumped the duffel bag inside, then climbed into the SUV.

Bolan turned the vehicle in the direction of the

distant highway, his mind working constantly. He
needed to get them clear of this area, somewhere they
could hole up temporarily and assess the events that
had started when Erika Dukas had received a phone
call from a friend sometime earlier that day.

2

Earlier that day—Falls Church, Virginia

Chill winds had been blowing from the north with a hint of snow in the fine rain misting the windshield of Erika Dukas's 1965 Chevrolet Impala-SS. She drove steadily, aware of the gathering weariness that had started to impinge upon her being as she wound down. She had just finished a complicated translation for Carmen Delahunt at Stony Man Farm. The work had been intense, urgent. After handing over the completed transcript, she had logged out and had left the Farm, raising a hand to the blacksuit manning the exit gate. She had maneuvered the Impala along the quiet roads until she was able to pick up the main highway that would take her home.

Home was an apartment in Falls Church, Fairfax County. It wasn't a long drive, but tiring on this gray winter afternoon. The constant rain didn't help, the insistent sweep of the wipers across the windshield doing little to help her relax. She put on the radio and picked up some soft jazz. The car's heater blew warm air around her feet. A couple of times Dukas had to blink her eyes. She was tired. She hadn't been home for two days. The anticipation of a relaxing shower and bed filled her thoughts.

Once inside her apartment she switched on the lights, dropped her briefcase by the door and shrugged out of her coat. Making her way to the kitchenette, she filled the kettle with fresh water and clicked it on to boil. She spooned coffee into a mug, kicked off her shoes as she wandered across to her telephone and then checked her messages.

There were four.

One from her mother asking when she was going to visit.

A call from someone wanting to sell her insurance.

And two from a longtime girlfriend Dukas hadn't spoken to for a while. The first was from the day before, the second from a few hours earlier.

The girl was Tira Malivik. And the first thing Dukas noticed was the fear in her voice. She couldn't explain it any other way. Her friend was frightened of something, and she was reaching out for help.

Dukas snatched up the phone and hit the speed-dial button for Malivik's cell number. She waited as it rang. Finally the call was answered.

"Tira? It's me—Erika. I just got your message. What's wrong?"

She could hear ragged breathing on the line and muted sounds in the background.

"Tira speak to me. I'm here. It's going to be all right. Please, talk to me."

"I think I've lost them for now. Jesus, Erika, they won't give up. I don't know what to do."

"Who? Who's after you?" Dukas asked.

"—want something. But I don't have it. I sent it on—"

Her voice faded and Dukas thought her friend was going to put the phone down.

"Listen to me, Tira. I'm going to come and get you. Just tell me where—"

"No! I can't do that. I'm sure they can hear. They'll know. I can't tell you where I am."

"The police—"

"Uh-uh. I can't trust anyone except you. Because you're my friend. Erika, are you still my friend?"

"After what we've been through? Hey, I ate your cooking, remember? Just tell me where you want to meet," Dukas said, hoping to calm her friend's fear.

"One hour. At JR's."

"I'll be there."

The line went dead.

ERIKA LOCKED THE CAR AND hurried to the closest elevator in the garage. She waited impatiently until the doors opened and she was able to step inside, punching the button for the Lower Level Food Court. She was reminded how many times she had made this very trip to meet her friend. Whenever they were able to arrange a get-together it was at Union Station, where they would indulge themselves at Johnny Rockets Diner. Ignoring all the diet rules, they indulged in burgers, fries and shakes, enjoying a brief respite from the cares of their daily routines, sharing news, gossip and girl talk.

But this visit had no fun time on its agenda. As the elevator slowed, Dukas was full of doubt and concern. She stepped out and headed for the diner, scanning the food court for her friend, and wondered just what it was her friend had gotten herself into. She patted the inside pocket of her jacket, just to confirm her cell phone was still there.

She spotted Tira Malivik through the main window of the diner, sitting in their usual booth. They made eye contact and waved in recognition. Avoiding the press of people milling around the area, Dukas reached the door and pushed her way through. Immediately the familiar odors of food and coffee assailed her senses. There was a hum of voices and background music.

A vivacious, dark-haired young woman with striking good looks, Tira Malivik had undergone a dramatic change. As Dukas slid into the booth across from her she noticed the dark shadows beneath Malivik's eyes, the haggard expression on her face. Her usually shining hair was limp and tangled, and it looked as if she had been sleeping in her clothes. When she reached across to grasp Erika's hands, Malivik was shaking.

"What's wrong? And don't even suggest it's nothing," Dukas said.

"I wish I could lie about it."

Before they could continue a smiling waitress came

over. They ordered two large black coffees. As soon as the waitress left, Dukas turned back to her friend.

"Tell me, and don't leave anything out."

Dukas listened without interruption, except for when the coffee arrived, and by the time Malivik had finished, the Stony Man translator knew what she had to do.

"Your uncle Lec? Where is he now? And what about this package he sent you?"

"He asked me to get it somewhere safe. Out of the reach of the people looking for him."

"And did you?"

Malivik nodded, a ghost of a smile briefly edging her pale lips.

"Did he tell you what was in this package?"

"Not directly. He just said it contained information these people do not want exposed. If it is, a number of important individuals are going to go to jail, or worse."

"Where are these people?" Dukas asked.

"Some in Bosnia. Others here in the States."

"So you have no idea what the information actually is?"

"Not until I read an e-mail he managed to send me just before he dropped out of sight. I haven"t had time to check it out yet."

"First thing, we get you out of here. Somewhere you'll be safe until I can arrange protection. And not the police, or anyone we're not sure of," Dukas said.

"Can you do that?"

"Yes. The people I work for can do it. And you'll be more than safe with them. I promise."

Malivik clutched her coffee mug in both hands, drinking the hot liquid in quick gulps. She stared at Dukas. She was agitated.

"This is wrong. I shouldn't drag you into this. I'm sorry. Maybe I should go and you forget this meeting. These people are really scary, Erika."

"You should meet some of the people I work with," Dukas said, smiling. She took out her phone. "I'm going to help. Now I need to make a call. Look, you want more coffee? Something to eat?"

"No, but I need to go to the ladies' room."

"You go while I do this," Dukas said. "Hey, I know your e-mail address. Do I need a password?"

"I don't have my laptop with me."

"My people can access your site if they have the details. We need to read that message."

"Password is JRockets."

"Very subtle." Dukas laughed.

"I'm really sorry, Erika. I feel so bad doing this to you," Malivik said.

"Hey, I said no problem. Now go and let me call."

As she punched in the number that would connect her with Stony Man Farm, Dukas watched her friend cross the diner and push through the door to the ladies' room. She was concerned about the way she was acting. It was as if she wanted to get up and run. Her attention was diverted as her call was answered and she eventually found herself speaking to Barbara Price and explaining the situation.

"You listen to me," Price said. "You did right. I'll

set something up and get right back to you. I'll pass the e-mail details on. Take Tira to your place. As soon as you arrive call me, and we'll liaise. Hey, take it easy. Get your friend settled and wait for us."

"Thanks. I owe you," Dukas said.

"Oh, yes, and big-time too," Price said lightly.

Dukas drained her coffee mug. As she placed it on the table she thought Malivik had been gone too long.

She stood up and pushed her way through the crowded diner. She hadn't realized just how much it had filled up since her arrival. She wedged her way through until the reached the ladies' room and pushed open the door. Malivik wasn't there. She checked the cubicles twice. There was only one way in and one way out. As she walked back into the diner a chill coursed through her.

She checked out the restaurant, pushing back the panic edging its way to the surface. Back at the booth she met the waitress holding the check. Dukas paid it and turned to leave. She saw Malivik's purse still on the booth seat. She picked it up and weaved through the crowd. Outside she stood helpless, not sure which way to go. She wandered around for twenty minutes, searching, hoping her friend had just left the diner to get some air. She called Malivik on her cell phone, but the phone was switched off.

She gave up and went back to her car, deciding to check at her own place first to see if Malivik showed up there.

The weather had become worse, the falling rain bitterly cold as the temperature dropped.

"MISS DUKAS?"

She glanced up at the speaker. He was just behind her, to one side, a stocky man in a dark suit, his tie awkwardly knotted. He held out a black badge holder and flipped it open as soon as she gave him her attention, holding it where she could see it, rain speckling the metal shield. He had materialized from the shadows behind her as she bent to lock her car.

There was something in the too swift way he identified himself, a sense of not being quite who he claimed.

"I'm with WPD. I need you to come with me," he said.

"And why is that?"

"To help us verify an identification."

"For who?"

"A young woman involved in a traffic accident." The man was trying hard to stay professional. "I have a car over there."

Dukas hesitated, caution holding her back, and when the man reached out to touch her elbow she drew away.

"Why did you come to me?" she asked.

"She kept saying your name. Asking us to find you. We looked in her bag and found your address in her diary."

"Is it Tira?" Dukas asked, frightened.

"Tira Malivik could be her name, but we need formal identification."

"Nothing in her bag to prove who she is?" Dukas asked.

"No. Look, Miss Dukas, we need to go now. It is urgent."

I'm sure it is, she thought, considering I have Tira's bag in my hand right now.

She finished locking her car and fell in alongside the man as they walked in the direction of the waiting car, engine running, lights on. Dukas saw the dark outline of a driver. Her escort opened the back door.

There was no way she was getting in a car with these men.

About to step around the open door, Dukas allowed the bag to slip from her hand and as it hit the ground she caught it with her foot, pushing it under the door.

"Sorry," she said.

The man grunted, then bent to pick up the bag.

Dukas lunged forward, using her full body weight to slam the door into the man. The bulk of the door connected with his upper body, driving him against the inner frame. Erika grabbed the edge of the door and pulled it wide, then hit it again. The man had slumped to his knees and this time the door thudded into his skull. He uttered a low moan and sprawled on the wet ground.

Snatching up the bag, Dukas ran behind the car. As she moved she caught a glimpse of the driver's door swinging open. She knew the area well, so despite the driving rain she had no need to hesitate. She raced across the curving swell of the grassed area and into the landscaped bushes and trees. She followed the downward slope, the dark trees closing around her. Running hard, stumbling on the uneven ground, she weaved her way to the far side of the wooded area and came out just above the feeder road. Only then did she stop to catch her breath. She took a few moments to check out her surroundings, seeking any sign of movement.

Had they followed?

She saw no signs of movement.

So what now?

She couldn't risk going back to her apartment, or even to her car. Concern for her friend guided her. She eased her way along the fringe of the trees until she was well clear of the area, then made her way to the main road. She would hail a taxi and get over to Malivik's apartment.

IN THE CAB SHE CALLED Stony Man Farm and was more than relieved when Barbara Price answered.

"Hey, I've been worried. Where have you been?" Price said.

Dukas explained what had happened. "I'm checking Tira's apartment," she said. "I'm on my way there now. That help we talked about? I may need to take you up on it."

"Already sanctioned. Erika, maybe you should back off until we know what's going on," Price said.

"Look, it's been well over two hours since Tira went missing. I can't just stand back and do nothing. I'll be at her place in a few minutes. Barb, I have to do this. She's my best friend and she called on me for help. She has no one else."

"I don't think this is a good idea," Price said.

"I won't do anything stupid."

"Give me her address."

Dukas passed along the information, then ended the call before Price talked her out of what she intended. She was afraid of what she might find, but she was unable to ignore the fact her friend was in some kind of trouble.

3

The entrance to Malivik's building was reached by climbing a short flight of stone steps. Dukas got to the door without incident. Pushing inside she stopped in the lobby of the building aware of a sick feeling in her stomach. She considered the fact that she might be well out of her depth.

She climbed to the third floor apartment. No light showed under the door. Dukas took the keys from her friend's bag and opened the door. Through the gap she could see the room was in darkness, the gloom broken only by the pale light coming through the window. Dukas reached inside and clicked on the light. The room had been disturbed, furniture out of place and objects strewed across the floor.

And from behind the leather couch a bare arm, streaked with blood, jutted at an odd angle.

"Please no," she whispered. "Not Tira."

Her plea was too late. When she stepped around the couch, she immediately recognized her friend lying in a wide, congealing pool of dark blood.

She was naked. Her clothes slashed and cut away by

the same brutal blade that had ravaged her flesh, leaving her butchered and bloody. Her throat had been deeply cut, the flesh peeling back in a moist, glistening layer.

About to move toward the body, Dukas drew back. There was nothing she could do for her friend now.

Dukas reached into her pocket for her cell, then picked up a whisper of sound from the other side of the room. She realized she was not alone. She turned for the door, catching movement out the corner of her eye—a fast moving figure coming out of the bedroom, heading directly for her.

She reached the door and yanked it open. An arm snaked around her neck, the impact of her assailant's body pushing her into the door frame. She stumbled, pulling her attacker with her as he maintained his grip. On her knees, she threw out one hand to grip the door frame. She could feel warm breath on the back of her neck that drew her anger as she recalled everything that had happened—the men at her apartment, discovering her dead friend and now this unprovoked attack. It gelled into a moment of pure, reflex rage.

Dukas drove the back of her skull into her attacker's face. It hit hard and she heard him gasp, the arm around her neck loosening. She pulled free, pushing to her feet and turning to face the man. Still on his knees, temporarily engulfed in the blinding pain of his bruised nose, he was vulnerable. Dukas didn't hesitate. She raised her right foot and slammed the heel of her boot into his mouth. He fell back, his face bloody, and in that instant she turned and ran.

Dukas raced along the corridor to the stairs, almost throwing herself down the steep flights, trying not to think about what she had left behind. She reached the lobby, barely able to stop herself from crashing into the front door. She fumbled for the handle, pulling it wide, and faced a dark figure blocking the entrance as she went through.

She hadn't considered the man upstairs might have a partner.

Her forward rush took her headlong into the newcomer. His arms came up to grip her, but to steady her, not to imprison. Even in the flash of panic she knew to trust the voice when he spoke.

"Easy now, Erika, I'm on your side."

"She's dead. Tira's dead," Dukas cried.

She felt the man's hands on her shoulders. The gesture helped to calm her. He eased her around and she felt herself being guided to a corner of the lobby.

"I think he was still there. In her apartment," she said.

"Let me worry about him. You wait here."

"With more of them liable to come through the front door? I'll feel safer behind you."

Mack Bolan saw the determined expression in her eyes.

"Watch my back then," he said.

He eased the Beretta 93-R from his shoulder rig and held it against his right thigh as they started up the stairs, Bolan taking the lead.

Behind him Dukas offered directions and Bolan followed them. The apartment door stood ajar, the lights still on. As he reached the door, he saw the blood smear on the frame. Fresh blood was still seeping down the wood frame.

"You hurt?" he asked, indicating the blood.

"Not me, him," came the matter-of-fact reply.

He toed the door open, his gaze covering the interior. Even from the door he could see the bloodied arm jutting from behind the couch. Bolan reached out and pushed the door wide, senses tuned to pick up any sound from inside.

He did pick up something. Not from inside the apartment, but from the corridor—sudden movement. Dukas gasped as she became aware herself. Bolan turned, swinging the 93-R around. He saw two armed figures converging on the apartment, weapons up and ready.

He gave them credit for that. Whoever they were, they had been a step ahead. His first instinct was to protect Dukas, and he placed a firm hand on her shoulder and shoved her out of harm's way.

And then from inside the apartment another figure materialized from behind the open door, something in his raised right hand. Bolan sensed it swinging toward him, heard the whoosh of disturbed air. He tried to pull himself aside, but the heavy object slammed down across his right shoulder, numbing it. He was barely able to keep a grip on the Beretta. His attacker muttered in frustration, swung the club again and this time connected with Bolan's skull. The blow drove Bolan to his knees. The third blow put him facedown on the carpet and every light in Washington went out.

THE EXECUTIONER'S AWARENESS RETURNED gradually. His initial conscious reaction was to the savage pulse of pain inside his skull. It occupied his elusive thoughts and he remained still, some deep instinct telling him to assess prior to acting.

He played dead, accepting that it was a disturbing analogy. His first cogent thought centered on Erika Dukas. Where and how was she? It was something he would need to verify very soon.

He began to filter in extraneous sound and movement. Low talk. Casual movement.

He cracked open an eye, saw the world come slowly back into focus.

He was still in Tira Malivik's apartment, lying against one wall. The first thing he made out was the couch. Tira Malivik's body had been behind it, but the body had been moved and the couch dragged forward to cover the bloodstain.

A man was lounging on the couch, staring at the television, the sound turned low. A second man wandered into view, a filled glass in one hand. From the way the pair was acting Bolan guessed they were on their own. He didn't dismiss the possibility of there being others, maybe in one of the other rooms—maybe keeping watch over Dukas.

The man on the couch rose and crossed the room to stand over Bolan. He saw the man had a bloody nose and a cut around his mouth.

"Hey, Kimble, maybe you hit this asswipe too hard," the man said. His voice was slightly blurred due to his injured mouth.

"Do I look as if I care?"

"I mean he might not be able to talk. Billingham isn't going to be pleased about that," the first man replied.

Two names so far, Bolan thought. Kimble. Billingham.

One paid help, the other the ringmaster.

"Get him on his fuckin' feet," Kimble said. "I'll make him talk."

The nameless man hauled Bolan upright with ease. Bolan could feel the toned muscle under the man's street clothes. There was strength there. The Executioner offered no resistance. He was not quite ready to make his own physical contribution yet. The man dragged him to the couch and dumped him with little grace.

Kimble reached behind himself and produced Bolan's Beretta. He leaned over and rapped the muzzle against Bolan's cheekbone. "C'mon sleeping beauty. Talk time."

Bolan opened his eyes and stared up at Kimble. He held his gaze and despite his bravado—and the gun— it was Kimble who broke contact.

Bolan pushed himself into a sitting position. "Is the woman all right?" he asked directly.

"Hey, it speaks," Kimble crowed.

"Well?" Bolan said.

"Don't get pushy. We ask, you answer," Kimble said.

"Right now your priority is thinking 'bout yourself," the other man said. "Like how long you might stay alive."

"Is she okay?" Bolan asked again.

"Jesus, this freak has a one-track mind."

"Yeah, well, his ID has him down as some kind of Justice agent," Kimble said. "You know what that means. They're just fancy cops, and cops have simple minds."

"The woman," Bolan persisted.

"Christ," Kimble said. "Look, pal, she ain't here. Right now she's fine, but how long depends on the way she answers some questions."

The other man reached into the pocket of his dark pants and produced a switchblade. He pressed the button and the slim, shining blade snapped into position. His face took on a sudden change, his mouth tightening into a thin line as he flexed his muscles.

Kimble reached in a pocket and produced a bundle of plastic ties. "Let's get this done."

No time for working on a strategy. Bolan saw the lines of engagement change. Talk was over. He came up off the couch, fighting back the wave of nausea that rose within him.

Bolan's right foot swept up, and the toe of his shoe drove into the knife wielder's groin. The blow was without mercy, delivered with every ounce of strength the Executioner could muster. The man made a high-pitched squeal of pain. The kick stalled him long enough for Bolan to continue his move, his body swiveling so that he came face-to-face with the startled Kimble. Bolan's hands reached out and caught the Beretta by the barrel. He twisted and pulled, hearing Kimble's trigger finger snap.

Kimble howled as Bolan shouldered him aside, turning about to face the nameless man. The big man, one hand clutching at his groin, was already on the move, lurching in Bolan's direction. The glittering switchblade was slashing the air as he closed in. Bolan raised the 93-R and pulled the trigger. The Beretta chugged a 3-round burst, the 9 mm slugs punching into the man's chest. He twisted away from Bolan, dropping to his knees, then went facedown on the carpet. He jerked a few times before subsiding with a long, harsh sigh.

Turning away, Bolan made Kimble the focus of his attention, making sure the man could see the unwavering muzzle of the Beretta.

Kimble panicked. This was not how it was supposed to go down.

Moving behind him, Bolan closed an arm around Kimble's neck, tight enough to make the man struggle for air. He put the muzzle of the Beretta against the side of the man's head and pressed hard, letting the warm metal gouge a raw circle in his flesh.

"Think about this, Kimble. Your buddy is dead. You saw how quick it happened. Consider that when you start to answer my questions," Bolan said.

He let the man think about it for a while. Bolan slackened his grip on Kimble's neck and the man sucked air in greedily, like a swimmer escaping drowning. He maintained pressure on the Beretta's muzzle, making sure Kimble stayed aware of his precarious position.

"Simple question. Where do they have the woman?" the Executioner asked.

Kimble knew his life depended on his reply. He was under no illusions. He had seen how easily this man had killed his partner and knew that same fate awaited him if he failed to give the right information.

"If I tell you, can we make a deal?" he asked.

Bolan didn't answer. Instead he dug the muzzle of the Beretta deeper into Kimble's flesh, turning it enough to break the skin. Kimble felt the warm trickle of blood from the tear.

"Where do they have the woman?"

"No deal, huh? Look, what if I send you to a certain address and she isn't there?" Kimble asked.

"Then I'll come back and we'll start over. You aren't going anywhere, Kimble. So make certain I hit the correct location," the Executioner warned.

"If my people find out I sent you, I'm dead anyway. They'll come after me."

"No, they won't. I can promise you that."

The tone was neutral but the implication was clear. Kimble knew if this man went after the woman, it wouldn't matter who stood in his way.

Bolan stepped away from Kimble and stood facing him, the Beretta still trained on the man.

"Your choice, Kimble. Give me what I want, and I'll cut you a break. Screw me, and you'll wish I'd killed you right here and now."

Kimble stared into the cold blue eyes and he saw his own fate mirrored there.

"You genuine on that? Leaving me alive I mean?"

"I never lie, Kimble."

There was something in the guy's voice that made Kimble believe him.

"Then we have a deal."

Bolan gestured with the pistol and walked Kimble across the room. He made him sit on the floor next to the heavy radiator piped into the wall, then picked up the plastic ties Kimble had let drop to the floor. He handed one to Kimble.

"Around your ankles. Make sure it's tight."

"Jesus, my finger's broke. How can I—"

"Your choice, Kimble. I still have bullets in this gun."

Bolan waited until Kimble did as he was instructed, then fashioned a loop with a second plastic strip. He bound Kimble's wrists together, then took more strips and secured the bound man to the thick steel pipe running from the radiator to the solid floor.

"Now tell me where she is and how many are with her."

When Bolan had the information locked down he rose to his feet, holstering the Beretta, then turned to leave.

"Hey," Kimble called, "how do I get out of this?"

"If the information is genuine, I won't be back. I'll leave a message with my people to come and get you."

Kimble's anger burst like an unchecked flood.

"You fuckin' told me you don't lie. I give you what you want, and you toss me to the cops? What kind of a deal is that?"

"It's what we agreed, Kimble. You give me the right words, I don't kill you. That stands. I didn't say anything about letting you walk away from this."

Bolan paused to stare the man down. "You want to re-negotiate the terms? You still have nine fingers left."

Kimble fell silent, figuring he'd worked the best deal he was likely to get. He watched the tall man leave, and reasoned he was better off where he was. He didn't envy the snatch crew. He tried not to imagine what was going to happen when the unexpected visitor showed up at the abandoned farmhouse.

4

Their bodies chilled beneath their wet clothing, they climbed out of the SUV and crossed to the motel cabin Bolan had booked them into. The night clerk had viewed Bolan with suspicion when he had stepped into the office, muddy and wet.

"Heck of a night," Bolan said. "Car skidded off the road into a ditch. Hit my head on something. Took me an hour to get it back out. Lucky for me she's a four-by-four. Truth is, I'm too tired to drive any farther tonight. Wife is too. You got a double room with plenty of hot water?"

The night clerk looked the big man up and down, figuring he wasn't going to throw him out. Not the size he was. When Bolan produced a credit card and handed it over, the clerk saw no further problems. He processed the card and gave Bolan the key to one of the empty cabins. In truth all the cabins were empty, Bolan had noticed, seeing the key board was full. The night clerk decided at least one cabin taken was better than none at all. It had been a bad day all-round, with the lousy weather and the forecast for possible snow sweeping down from the north. He blamed the Canadians for that. *Why couldn't they keep their damn snow up in Alaska, or wherever they stored it?*

Bolan unlocked the cabin door and they went in. He dropped the bag holding his weapons on the floor. He closed the door and secured it as Dukas clicked on the lights. The room looked comfortable and the heat was on.

Bolan was ready to call in to the Farm and give them an update, but he pushed that aside when he heard subdued sobbing suddenly coming from Dukas. She had gone to stand at the window, leaning her forehead against the glass. He could see her shoulders moving as she wept, and he felt her anguish. Bolan crossed over quietly and stood behind her, resting a hand on her shoulder.

She turned to face him.

"This has been a nightmare. Things like this don't happen to people like me," she said. "I translate languages. I don't kill people."

"Circumstances sometimes don't allow us the privilege of choice. I'm sorry you got pulled in at the deep end, Erika. You answered a friend's cry for help, and now you're caught in the middle. What happened back there—none of us wanted it."

"How do you deal with it? How do you forget when it happens to you all the time?" Dukas knew the man who'd introduced himself as Matt Cooper was some kind of special agent who'd been sent by Barbara Price.

"I don't forget," he said. "I have my ghosts and they come back to visit me every so often."

"That man was going to kill you. I saw that and I couldn't let it happen. But—"

"You did what you had to. No guilt in that."

"I took a life," she said.

"If he had gunned me down, *you* would have been next. You defended *your* right to live. That's a natural reaction."

She stared up into his steady blue eyes, seeing not savagery, nor the cold heart of a merciless man, but the gaze of someone who carried compassion for those who needed it, and at that moment she was in need. She leaned forward, wanting his strength, and he slid his arms around her as she rested her head against his chest, holding him tight against her. Bolan could feel her trembling and he remained where he was, holding her until she had settled.

She took a deep breath, then she raised herself on her toes and kissed him on the cheek before letting go.

Bolan saw sudden concern in her eyes. "Erika?"

"You," she said. "You've got a bad gash on your head. Where they clubbed you at Tira's apartment. Remember?"

Bolan did, reaching up to touch the spot that was still bleeding.

"Told the desk clerk I hit my head when the car went off the road."

"Go sit down. I'll find something to clean it up." She stared at him. *"Do it."*

Bolan did as he was told.

She brought a towel from the bathroom and cleaned

up the gash as best she could. When she was done she filled the room's kettle and plugged it in the electrical outlet while she prepared coffee. They sat silently drinking and for a time there was a fragile peace.

Bolan found a pair of white bathrobes in sealed plastic laid out on the bed. He passed one to Dukas.

"Take the first shot in the bathroom," he said.

"Don't think I won't," she said.

Bolan pulled his cell phone from the pocket of his mud-streaked jacket and called Barbara Price.

"Run these names through the system," he said to the Stony Man mission controller. "Billingham. Somebody important. Other is a perp named Kimble. I'd guess he has a rap sheet. I expect he's no more than a hired gun. See what comes up."

"Hey, how are you two doing?" Price asked.

"I'd say we've both had better days."

"Any light at the end of the tunnel?"

"Still digging."

"Erika?"

"They killed her friend Tira. Erika found her. She's coping," Bolan said.

"That translates as covering it up well," Price replied.

"I've got it covered."

"Look after my girl."

"Yes, Mama," Bolan said.

"I'll call when we get something on these names."

Bolan closed the phone. He could hear Dukas moving around the bathroom, and he thought about the remark Price had made about him looking out for the young woman. He was conscious of his responsibility for her. It was uppermost in his mind. Her safety was at the top of his list.

The bathroom door opened and Dukas appeared. She had changed into the bathrobe and looked slightly less stressed.

"All yours," she said.

Bolan picked up Tira Malivik's bag and handed it to her.

"Check it out," he said. "See if you can find anything."

She held the bag, hesitating, and Bolan could see the hurt in her eyes.

"It's like invading her privacy."

"No. It's helping to find out who took her from you. She was your friend, and I don't think Tira would feel you were doing anything wrong," Bolan said.

Dukas opened the bag and tipped the contents across the bed. As she started to go through them she heard the bathroom door close.

She still felt a trace of unease going through her friend's possessions. Most of the items were mundane, everyday female things. Dukas pushed this aside and concentrated on what remained.

A slim leather wallet. She examined the contents: just under a hundred dollars in bills, various credit cards, driver's license. There were some folded receipts. She glanced at them, placing them aside as she read each one.

She found one issued by the U.S. Postal Service. The date was from a few days earlier. The receipt was for the mailing of a *package* to be delivered and held at a specific destination.

When Dukas read the delivery destination, she smiled. *"Very smart, Tira,"* she whispered. *"Clever move."* She crossed to the bathroom door and knocked.

"Problem?" Bolan asked.

"No. But I just found out where the *package* is."

"Give me a minute."

Bolan emerged from the bathroom, dressed in the other robe and toweling his hair. Dukas was at the window, staring at the still falling rain. She turned when she caught Bolan's reflection in the glass.

"Tira mailed the package away for safety. She sent it to Maple Lake, Colorado. It's a small town in the mountains. Pretty well off the beaten track. Depends on tourists in summer. This time of year it more or less shuts down."

"What's the connection?" Bolan asked.

"Our families used to go there for vacations. Rented the same lodge every time. It's where Tira and I first met when we were teenagers. Up until a couple of years ago we still managed to visit on and off."

She made them both fresh mugs of coffee. Bolan waited until she sat down again.

"Tell me about Tira."

"I've known her for maybe fifteen years. We shared an apartment for three. She is…she was my friend. The past few years we saw less of each other because she worked for an international aid agency and traveled a lot to Bosnia. It's where her family originally came from. She still has relatives there." Dukas glanced across at Bolan. "Do you think this could have anything to do with her work?"

"Right now we're trying to figure that out," he said.

"Tira did mention one person in particular. Her uncle. His name was Pavlic. Lec Pavlic. He lived in Sarajevo. When she was over there a couple of months back, he kept trying to contact her but she only managed to see him one time. She was due to ship out on some assignment. She said he seemed very agitated. He told her there was something he needed to discuss with her. *Very important*, he said. The only other contact she had with him was a call on her cell phone. Pavlic said he was hoping to get to the U.S. shortly, and he had to see her. She gave him her address and phone number. They were going to get together when he came." She fell quiet for a moment, then looked Bolan in the eye. "What is it that Lec Pavlic involved her in?"

5

Bosnia

Lec Pavlic had known this day would come—when greed and ambition outgrew loyalty. A day when mistrust finally showed its ugly face and sides were taken. Sometime back he had envisaged and prepared his escape plan, though hoping he might never have to use it. His suspicions were roused when he began to be left out of meetings, was passed over when better positions became available within the consortium. His advice became less sought after, and conversations dried up whenever he entered a room. He knew well enough not to ask direct questions simply because denial would only reinforce his concerns. So he stayed silent, observed and let the evidence grow. It took him some time before he actually got a line on what was happening. When he did he was shocked, but not entirely surprised, because over the years there had been a few disappearances of fringe members of the consortium, in Bosnia and the United States. Two of the men who had done the actual killing had already died. A third had barely survived an automobile accident that had left him fully paralyzed and in a coma. Jev Ritka's accident had occurred recently. Murmurings of disquiet had been raised.

Looking back, he realized that his misgivings had been well-founded. At the time, his financial acumen had been sought after. His manipulative skills with money made him an important member of the exclusive group, and he had no qualms in going along with the devious and violent nature of the operation. During the formative years, Pavlic had been privy to everything, but as time went by he realized he was being cut out of certain aspects of the operation. At first he paid little attention. He had more than enough to keep him busy and he shouldered his responsibility. But the increasingly ruthless manner in which matters were pursued and the way new blood was brought in began to bother him. It dawned on him that he was being sidelined, edged out, albeit stealthily, and by ways so subtle he might have missed them. But he *didn't* miss them and began to take a deeper interest in the day-to-day operations. He did it carefully, gaining scraps of information, picking up snippets of conversation, until he had satisfied himself that he was being pushed out.

Then he knew what he had done all those years ago was going to pay off.

Pavlic had always tempered actions with extreme caution. His profession nurtured the characteristic with a high degree of enthusiasm. Financial dedication engineered total observation of foresight. Noticing pitfalls meant avoiding them. Making provisions for possible hazards encouraged all forms of insurance against those hazards.

When the consortium's scheme had been close to fruition and they were all committed, Lec Pavlic, ever diligent, had considered his options.

His friend, a struggling businessman who ran a video filming company, possessed the qualities Pavlic needed. Hac Tivik had no morals and even better he would do anything for money. Over a meal and several bottles of wine, Tivik listened to Pavlic's proposal. He professed some shock when Pavlic told him what the group had planned, but his outrage faded when Pavlic named the price he was willing to pay to have the incident recorded, with the promise of more at monthly intervals.

Even so, as time went by and people began to die, concern over his own mortality had caused sleepless nights and Pavlic began to walk carefully when he was in the presence of the group. He allowed his concerns to guide him. He watched and listened, and it was soon obvious that a small cadre of people had quietly formed. People who outwardly still operated for the group, but who were, in truth, steadily building their own power base. Digging a little deeper, he realized that they were well-connected with the Americans who had been part of the original group that had planned and carried out the executions.

Still without solid proof, Pavlic knew that these powerful figures were manipulating the operations in order to further build their own power and riches. It was as simple as that. He began to suspect that his own position was at risk because his work meant he had access to and even control over the financial operations of the whole consortium. He was able at the touch of a computer button to move around vast sums of money. He knew where all the accounts were—the secret deposits, the offshore and Swiss accounts. It was a great deal of responsibility to be in the hands of one man, and though he had been a party to the slaughter on that fateful day—he was just as guilty—he realized it would mean little to the egomaniacs who were gathering themselves for total control.

As part of his survival plan, he started to siphon off money for himself. It was relatively easy. Pavlic routed the amounts back and forth between accounts, paying off contracts, using various sources to launder the cash, then placed it in numerous systems. He set up a number of dummy accounts, retaining passwords and numbers, and over a period of three months acquired substantial holdings he would be able to access from anywhere in the world. He felt safe because he still had an ace in the hole. The videotape that would implicate the whole of the consortium. As long as he retained that, he knew there was no danger of his being compromised and any threat was minimized.

Pavlic decided to consolidate his safety net. He met with Tivik and told his friend of his concerns. Tivik panicked. He looked on the news as if it was a death sentence about to be carried out immediately.

"We are dead," he said. "Lec, we're finished."

"Only if we do what you're doing right now. We've survived all this time. If we stay calm, we can come out of this fine," Pavlic said.

"Easy to say." Tivik reached for the bottle of wine on the café table and filled his glass. His hand trembled when he raised the glass.

"Listen to me," Pavlic said. "We have something none of them know about. The video evidence. That's our insurance. As long as we have that, they won't do anything."

Tivik drained his glass, wiping his hand across his mouth.

"There's something you haven't thought about, Lec. You have the evidence, yes, but they don't know about it. And if they don't know about it, how can it be a threat to them?"

Pavlic smiled.

"I've considered that myself. I plan to send them a sample. Enough to make them realize it exists, and any further accidents will result in the full tape being forwarded to interested authorities. That should make them think. Because they won't know who sent it." Pavlic raised his own glass. "We sow the seeds of confusion among our enemies."

It was a thought that would remain just that. Things were about to occur that would banish that notion from Pavlic's mind as he found himself struggling against more important matters. Like preserving his own life.

In a parked car across the street a camera was

lowered and the photographer picked up a cell phone, quickly tapping in a number.

"I think we need to meet. Pavlic has been having an interesting conversation with that friend of his. Yes, Tivik. I have it on camera. Perhaps I'm being overly cautious but something worries me about that pair. Tonight? Of course. Eight o'clock? I'll be there."

Sarajevo

THE MEETING TOOK PLACE IN the apartment they always used for clandestine business.

When Karel Medusku arrived he saw that the other men were already assembled.

Milos Radin was a heavyset man, his thick hair streaked with gray, his coarse features offset by the expensive clothing he wore. Medusku had always considered the man out of place in civilized company. Radin was a peasant who sometimes allowed his base nature to show. Not that anyone would ever make any mention of such errors. There was latent violence lurking close to the surface, and Radin had little problem using that brutal streak if someone offended him. He was in charge of handling government contracts with regard to civic and military construction.

Maric Jatko oversaw the group's security. It was a vague description for a violent man who would crush someone underfoot if need be. He was a man with few morals and no hesitation when it came to dealing with any threat to the group.

Sev Malik was the negotiator. He had gained a great deal since the massacre and the subsequent political advancement.

As soon as they were all settled, Radin turned to Jatko.

"We all know why we are here. Jatko has raised concerns over Pavlic that require addressing."

Jatko handed out copies of the photographs he had taken of Pavlic's meeting with Tivik.

"This isn't the first meeting they've had. But the significance is that prior to these recent get-togethers they hadn't seen each other for a long time."

"I understand your concern, Maric, but are these meetings significant? Should it worry us?" Medusku asked.

"Pavlic only contacted Tivik after Ritka had his accident. And there is more," Jatko said. "We all know Pavlic has been unhappy because he has missed promotions."

"That's because there was nothing to promote him for," Radin said. "The man is just a money mover. He diverts and places our cash. And please don't tell me it is a skilled profession. In the end Pavlic is a bank clerk."

"A very accomplished bank clerk," Jatko said. "Clever enough to skim off some of our money and divert it to a number of secure accounts."

Radin's face darkened with rage. "When did this happen? More importantly how did it happen?"

"Over the past few months. I have had my own people running random checks on our computer systems. One of them came across some embedded files hidden in program codes. It was pure luck he spotted them. He did some careful investigation and traced them back to Pavlic," Jatko replied.

"Damn him. It seems we were right not to promote him."

Medusku cleared his throat, taking a sip of water from the glass on the table in front of him. "What kind of money are we talking about?"

"Our initial check itemized over three million U.S. Pavlic is converting everything he takes to U.S. currency."

"How could he do that without us knowing?" Medusku asked.

Jatko smiled at the ignorance of the question.

"Pavlic deals with vast amounts every day. With all we have going on money is flowing in and out all the time. The accounts are never at the same levels one day to the next. Unless you run a full, detailed accounting, there is little chance of noticing money has been taken out of the system."

"That little prick is stealing our money." Radin banged his large fist on the table. "I want him skinned alive for this."

"Are you forgetting something?" Malik finally spoke. "Pavlic was with us. He knows everyone who was there that day. He knows where the bodies are buried."

"So?" Radin said. "Once he's dead that knowledge is buried with him."

"Perhaps not," Jatko said. "I did some back checking on Tivik. We accessed his bank account. He has been receiving large monthly cash deposits from Pavlic. Those payments started immediately after the killings. For over ten years now Pavlic has been paying his friend."

"Why?" Medusku asked.

"My guess? Tivik provided a service for Pavlic in 1995." Jatko gazed across the table at Radin. "Do you know what Tivik does for a living?"

"I know nothing about this man. Why should I?" Radin was showing signs of mounting impatience. "Tell us, Maric. Who is this man?"

"Tivik is a professional cameraman." Jatko did not embellish his statement. He allowed the fact to work its own significance on the group.

Radin held his gaze, almost willing Jatko to deny what he had just suggested. But the gradual realization dawning in his eyes told Jatko he had understood the unspoken possibility. "They filmed it? Pavlic has it on tape?"

"Logic suggests that could have been the outcome of such a collaboration."

Radin spoke very quietly.

There was a collective sigh as each man in the group considered the implications.

"If this turns out to be true and the contents of such a document were exposed—" Malik said.

Radin held up a big hand. "Before we all commit ritual suicide, let us consider the options. First we have to establish whether this is true. If not, we simply have to deal with Lec Pavlic for stealing our money. If what

Maric has suggested is true, then we still have to deal with Pavlic, but from another angle. Our main objective will be to gain possession of this video evidence. Destroy that and we neutralize Pavlic's threat of exposure."

"And what do we do if this theoretical video has been copied and placed in unknown locations? Or with trusted friends?" Malik asked.

"Sev, I never realized you had such a vivid imagination." Radin turned his attention back to Jatko. "I don't have to tell you what needs doing. Drop everything else and concentrate on Pavlic and this man, Tivik. I want to know if your theory is sound. If it isn't, no harm done. I'm starting to believe you may have stumbled onto a truth hidden from us for too long. Find out. Maric, I don't care what you need to do to get your answers. But maintain a low cover."

Jatko nodded, pushed his chair back and left the room.

"You realize what this means if Maric is correct?" Medusku said. He had gone pale, sweat glistening on his face. "What they will do to us?"

Radin smiled. "I know exactly what will happen. Let's hope Maric is wrong. If he isn't, that's the time to start worrying. As long as Pavlic isn't scared into doing anything, we have the time to protect ourselves."

"There is no point wasting more time here." Malik stood up. "I have an early appointment tomorrow. Just keep me informed."

"I will," Jatko said.

As Malik left, Radin picked up his coat and stood looking down at Medusku. The man had not moved.

"Lock up when you leave," Radin said. "And don't make too much of this. As I said, if we handle it efficiently nothing will change. Pavlic can be made to vanish easily if the need arises."

"And if that does not happen?"

Radin shrugged. "You see only the black side of everything. Don't bleed until you have been cut."

By the time Radin reached his car the light had gone out in the third floor apartment. As he drove away, heading back toward the center of town, he tapped in a number on his cell phone.

"Twenty minutes. You know where," he said when Jatko answered.

THE CHILL WIND DROVE FINE RAIN across the empty lot. Jatko eased his car alongside Radin's and stepped out, turning up the collar of his thick coat. He leaned in the open window.

"Is everything all right?" Jatko asked.

"I'm worried about Medusku. I have a feeling he's not going to be able to handle this well."

"You think he might talk?"

"He might get panicky enough. But I'm more concerned that he might do something to himself if he broods for too long. Unfortunately, he has a conscience."

"It could be awkward for us if he did do away with himself," Jatko said.

"Exactly what I was thinking. If that did happen, we could find ourselves being asked embarrassing questions."

"You want me to deal with him?"

"Let's be careful about it. Monitor him first. See what he does. If his actions threaten us—"

Jatko nodded. "I understand. Milos, we could be looking at a difficult time."

"Only if we allow it to control us." Radin started his engine. "Work as normal in the morning. I'll call Billingham in Miami. We may need to fly over and talk to him. I'll see you then."

"Drive carefully," Jatko said and walked back to his own car.

LEC PAVLIC SAW MEDUSKU CROSSING the parking lot in his direction. There was something in the way the tall, lean figure moved that prompted Pavlic to adopt a defensive posture. He studied Medusku closely. The man looked as if he hadn't slept. His usually thin face was gaunt, with dark circles under his eyes. When he came to a halt no more than a few feet from Pavlic, he stabbed the air with a bony finger.

"Is it true? What I heard last night?"

Although Pavlic couldn't be sure what the man was talking about, he felt a chill run through him that had nothing to do with the cold weather. "I'm sorry, I have no idea what you are talking about."

"Don't treat me like an idiot." Medusku leaned in close and Pavlic could smell the alcohol on his breath. "We know what you have been doing. Skimming money off the accounts into your own. Stealing from your comrades."

"Go home, Karel, you've been drinking."

"Does it surprise you? After what I learned last night?"

"Some nonsense about me taking money?" Pavlic found himself denying the accusation. What else could he do? He needed to get away from Medusku. To work out what he needed to do—and do it quickly.

Medusku tried to gain some dignity. He pulled himself upright, swaying a little. "It's more than the money, you bastard." His voice dropped to a conspiratorial whisper. "We know about the video—how you betrayed us even on that day."

Before more words were exchanged a dark figure appeared, crossing the lot in determined strides. It was Jatko. He walked up to Medusku and caught hold of his arm.

"What's going on here?" he demanded.

"Ask your drunken friend," Pavlic said. "Making a damn fool of himself. He should go have a nap. I have to go. I'm going to be late for my appointment."

Pavlic turned and climbed into his car. He drove off without a backward glance, leaving Jatko struggling with Medusku.

"And what was that all about?" Jatko asked, steering Medusku toward the office complex. "What the hell have you been saying?"

"Nothing of importance."

"Really? Is that why Pavlic looked so scared? Have you forgotten what we decided last night? To deal with this quietly. Not call attention to ourselves by arguing in a fucking parking lot."

"If we don't do anything, Pavlic could expose us," Medusku said.

"He might do that if drunken idiots start provoking him." Jatko maneuvered Medusku into one of the elevators, and they rode to the top floor and Radin's office suite.

Radin was on the phone. He glanced across at Jatko, then to the flushed and unsteady Medusku.

"Something has come up that requires my immediate attention. I will call you back." He cut off the call and stood up. "What's happened?"

PAVLIC DROVE DIRECTLY TO HIS apartment and called Tivik.

"Listen and don't interrupt. They may have found out about the video. We could be in trouble. We have to get out before they decide to move against us. You know what to do?"

"Yes," Tivik said.

Pavlic hung up. He went to his computer and accessed the accounts, using the passwords he controlled. He activated a program that wiped everything, including the data on the hard drive. He packed a bag, taking only a few items of clothing. Anything he might need later he could buy. Despite the situation he smiled. He didn't need to worry about money. He had plenty—and the disk he had in his possession would bring him more if he needed it. And he still had access codes to the group's bank accounts. He considered the possibility that once his disappearance became known the codes might be changed, shutting him out. It would be a nuisance but not the end of the world.

A half hour later he was in a taxi on his way to the airport. He sat back and watched the drab outline of the city slip behind him in the gloom. France first, then on to America. The U.S.A. was so large and diverse he would be able to lose himself easily.

The taxi turned into the airport. Pavlic glanced at his watch. Plenty of time before his flight. Once he was in the air he would be able to relax. In a few hours he would be in France, able to enjoy a good meal and a bottle of wine. From there he would book a flight to Washington.

He opened the slim case he was carrying. He had documentation related to his work and a slim laptop. He had enough identification to show he was a legitimate businessman going on a trip to the French capital. He had contacts in Paris, as he did in London and New York. In that respect he was legitimate.

In the attaché case, among other items, was a leather case holding CDs. They were data disks concerned with finance, business projections, details of share holdings. One was marked New Financial Year Estimates. If anyone opened the disk that was exactly what they would see. However, if they accessed an encrypted file they would see a copy of the video Tivik had filmed. Pavlic's friend, poor businessman though he might be, was a gifted technician when it came to handling the techniques of his craft.

It had been Tivik who had suggested transferring

the video to high-definition digitized disk. The carefully preserved tape cassette, kept in a controlled environment in his studio situated beneath his country lodge, had still been in good condition and Tivik had engineered the transfer using expensive equipment Pavlic had financed. It allowed Tivik to make a pristine copy, even enhancing and cleaning up the images. The end result was a copy that clearly identified the conspirators.

That copy was with him now and as long as he kept it away from Radin and the others, Pavlic felt reasonably secure.

It was early evening when he boarded his flight to France. A certain sense of relief washed over him the moment the plane took off. He watched the lights below fade into the darkness.

JATKO SPENT MOST OF THE afternoon attempting to track down Lec Pavlic. No one seemed to have any idea where he was. It was not until he managed to pull in his best IT operator that a picture began to emerge.

Erik Dupré, French by birth, had worked for Jatko for three years. "Well, I have one piece of news you won't like," the computer operator said.

Jatko shrugged. "The way today is going I wouldn't expect anything less."

"I accessed the financial database. Earlier today two million dollars U.S. was moved out of our accounts. I managed to follow the transactions only until they were diverted into unknown accounts. These cannot be accessed without passwords and account numbers. I will try again when I have more time."

"As soon as you are able, lock Pavlic out of our accounts. Change codes, passwords. I don't want him taking any more of our money," Jatko ordered. "Pavlic seems to have disappeared. He took a trip but left his car behind. A taxi perhaps?"

Dupré thought for a moment, then turned to his keyboard, fingers busy. "I checked his phone records. A taxi was sent to his address late this afternoon. Destination the airport. I'll check to see if he booked a ticket. If he did, he probably used a credit card. Shouldn't be too hard to find out."

It took Dupré only a short time to locate Pavlic's credit card account, using a backdoor program. He checked for the current listing and came up with Pavlic's flight booking.

"The good news is he's using his own card. Now that I have details we can follow him wherever he goes. If he's decided to run on the spur of the moment, he'll have to use his current cards. There's no way of changing them in the short term."

"The not so good news?" Jatko asked.

"By now he's an hour into his flight to Paris." He wrote something on a slip of paper. "Flight number and arrival time."

"Damn," Jatko said. "He's moving fast. Erik, keep on him. We have his cell phone number, so monitor any calls he makes. I need to know where and when. Understand?"

Dupré nodded.

Jatko returned to the main office. He went directly to Radin's desk and picked up one of the phones, tapping in a number. While he waited for it to connect he spoke to Radin.

"He's on his way to Paris. Flight left an hour ago."

His call was answered. "Yes? Berko? Listen, he's on his way to you." He recited the flight number and touchdown time Dupré had given him. "Tail him for now. We'll decide what to do next." Jatko hung up the phone. "We're tracking him," he said, smiling, and Medusku, watching from the far side of the room, felt a chill. He had seen that expression before, and it was anything but pleasant. "In the meantime I think we should pick up Tivik. See what he has to say."

6

Bolan's cell phone rang. It was Barbara Price.

"We accessed Tira Malivik's e-mail program and found the message from her uncle. He told her to make sure the *package* he mailed to her was kept safe. There was information in it that could identify a group of people, including himself, who was responsible for a crime in Bosnia over ten years ago. Those people knew he'd taped the incident and they're after him. The evidence could identify them all, including a couple of Americans. His plan was to get to the U.S. and collect the disk from Tira."

"Those people got to Tira first. And they connected Erika because Tira had spoken to her," Bolan said.

"That looks like the way it happened. We checked those names. You were right about Kimble. He did wet work for hire. But this is where it gets interesting. The name Billingham threw up a few leads, but the most likely is Thorne Billingham. Big in U.S. and international finance. Construction. Arms industry. Has friends in D.C. He's well connected. You name it, Billingham is there. He has links to Bosnia. He was involved in the reconstruction period after the conflict, around 1995. There was a lot of money thrown around then. And there were opportunities to make the kind of alliances that built careers."

"You figure Pavlic and Billingham have a past together?" Bolan asked.

"Yes. Pavlic is a moneyman, part of a conglomerate that came together just as the Bosnia conflict ended. We've got a couple more names as well. Milos Radin, a tough cookie by all accounts. He runs the Bosnian arm of the group and is a buddy of Billingham, it seems. Maric Jatko runs security for Radin. Exsecret police type. Nothing nice in his file. I'd put him down as one of the really bad guys."

"Keep me informed, Barb," Bolan said.

"That sounds suspiciously like you have something planned."

"I'm working on it. Just keep me posted on updates."

"Will do."

"Do one more thing. I need to talk to Jack. Soon." He ended the call.

Dukas had been listening to Bolan's end of the conversation, putting her own slant on what she'd heard. "I'm assuming there's nothing good coming from that conversation?"

"Some pointers as to who might be involved. And the fact that the *package* is the key. The people who went after Tira want it back. Badly enough to kill to get it. They figure you can lead them to it."

"Knowing where Tira sent it, I can. And that puts me smack in the middle of this."

"Then I need to get to it first."

"No. We need to get to it. Don't you even think about leaving me behind, Cooper. Do that, and I'll be on the next plane to Maple Lake."

"I'm too tired to argue. I guess you've earned the right to come along. *We'll* go and collect the *package*."

"Who do we call once we have the package? The cops? FBI?" Dukas asked.

Bolan shook his head.

"Intel suggests the U.S. end of this group has connections that go deep. That *could* include law enforcement and agency people. So until we know better we don't trust anyone out of our circle."

Dukas stared at Bolan. "Not so long ago my life was pretty simple. Now I'm in *X-Files* country. I've been kidnapped. Had to shoot someone and run for my life. This might be a normal day at the office for you, but it surely isn't for me."

Bolan nodded and squeezed her shoulder gently.

"So how about that trip to Colorado, Miss Dukas? I hear it's quiet this time of year."

7

"You have a good flight?"

Thorne Billingham, Milos Radin's American counterpart, watched the man as he entered the main cabin of the expansive motor cruiser. The cabin was luxuriously appointed, with smooth wood and hand-crafted leather.

While Radin was still in his suit, even wearing a tie, Billingham sported light, casual wear. The bright shirt hung easily on his hard body. Physically, they were alike. Tall men, powerfully built, they carried themselves with the ruthless assurance of total confidence in their abilities and the way they controlled their affairs.

Billingham was aware of a crisis, but nothing had been said when Radin had called to say he was on his way. Billingham had arranged for a vehicle to take Radin and his party from the landing strip west of Miami to the marina.

Radin looked fresh despite the long flight, though Billingham noticed faint shadows beneath his eyes. Radin settled in one of the comfortable leather recliners.

As the motor cruiser eased away from the busy

marina and headed out into the Gulf. Billingham sat down, facing his partner. "I'm listening," he said.

"Lec Pavlic had someone filming the executions. He has us all on tape. We found out by sheer luck. Jatko stumbled onto it. We checked it out, and it has now been fully confirmed. Before we pinned it down, Pavlic disappeared. We tracked him to France, then found out he had taken a flight here to the U.S. Jatko got to Pavlic's partner, Hac Tivik, the man who made the tape, and they extracted a confession. They also located the original tape, but it seemed that a copy had been digitalized and burned onto a disk. The disk was couriered to an address in Washington, to Pavlic's niece, Tira Malivik."

Billingham received the news with a degree of calm that impressed Radin. The American pushed to his feet and went to the bar where he poured himself a tumbler of bourbon, then resumed his seat.

"You've seen the tape?"

"Yes. Every one of us is clearly identified," Radin said.

"Did you keep the tape?"

"Once it was confirmed as genuine I destroyed it myself. I wasn't about to take the chance it might fall into the wrong hands."

"This cameraman. How did you deal with him?"

"Jatko persuaded him to talk. I am satisfied that the only copies of the evidence, apart from the disk Pavlic has, were the ones he hid in his cellar studio under his lodge."

"All that was dealt with?"

"It appears there was an unfortunate fire at Tivik's lodge. It was totally destroyed. Tivik's body would have been found in the ashes."

"Good. Now, who came with you?" Billingham asked.

"Jatko, of course. Eric Dupré. He is our IT expert. Brilliant with computers. He will be extremely useful. Jatko brought his two top security people. And Karel Medusku. I left Malik back home to watch over things."

"Why have you brought Medusku?"

Radin leaned back in his chair.

"He's not handling this well. The day after we met to discuss the matter he had a confrontation with Pavlic. I think it's what caused Pavlic to run. It ruined our chance of dealing with him quietly. I feel safer having Medusku close by so we can watch him."

"Then we keep watching him, Milos. If he constitutes any danger, we deal with him. Agreed?"

"Yes."

Billingham went quiet for a time, his mind working busily.

"Pavlic. You never do know about people," he said. "I always had him down as a sly son of a bitch, but I never figured him to be so imaginative."

"He had us all fooled. Not just about the tape," Radin said.

"Christ, what else has he been up to?"

"Jatko found out he was manipulating assets. Working on his own. He set up dummy accounts and siphoned off large cash amounts. Over four million. We have been unable to access those accounts."

"He probably decided we couldn't touch him even if we found out," Billingham said, "I take it Pavlic is in the video himself?"

"Yes."

"He's let more than ten years pass without stepping forward as a witness against us. Do you see him as a martyr risking prison by admitting he was part of it? And as someone who has profited as well?"

"Not really," Radin said.

Billingham smiled. "Pavlic has backed himself into a corner. Caught whichever way he wriggles." He rose, striding across to stare out across the lazy swell of the Gulf. "Ten years," he said, for the first time allowing bitterness to creep in. "Ten fucking good years and still getting better. Has Pavlic got any idea how deeply I'm tied to alliances and deals? The people I run with? Especially Ramsey Granger. He's going to flip when I tell him his face is on that film along with the rest of us. Milos, I'm damned if I'm going to let that little prick Pavlic ruin it all. He'll give up that evidence before we bury him. And that is a promise I'll keep."

Granger Industries, California

"MY GOD, THORNE, THIS WILL damage my organization if it comes out. You know the level of government I deal with. My company has a high-profile relationship with the military. If it comes out I built my business on the proceeds of money stolen from the Bosnian re-construction funding a lot of people could fall. Some of them way over my head. Christ, think of the favors given. Campaign funding taken from the postconflict pot. It would feed the media for months."

"Ramsey, we went into this with our eyes wide open. We *did* the deed," Billingham said.

"Don't fucking remind me, Thorne. I know what we did. We all got our hands bloodied that day. What I didn't expect was Pavlic filming it for prime time on *Sixty Minutes*." Granger drew a breath. "You know what galls me? The times I've had that asshole as a dinner guest at my home. He sat there eating my food and joking with me, and all the time he had that tape. I guess I have to give him brownie points for his nerve."

"Ramsey, we're closing in on him. One way or another we're going to get our hands on that disk *and* Pavlic."

"Just listen for a minute," Granger snapped. "I can back any move you make. Let me know what you need. Men, equipment, anything. Find Pavlic. We need that disk."

"We're on it, Ramsey. As soon as we have definite information, I'll pass it along."

Granger hung up. He was sweating. He was just glad Billingham couldn't see that. Bravado over the telephone was one thing. In truth he was nervous. Ten years on, and so much had happened. They had all gained status and wealth, cultivated relationships that had enriched their lives. Granger walked the corridors of power in Washington, in London, in Paris. He knew people. If the sordid details came out about that day of…it had been so long since he had even thought about it he found it hard to put a word to the act.

Murder?

Slaughter?

A necessary execution?

However it was described, it wouldn't sit comfortably within Granger's circles. It didn't take a great deal to imagine the expressions on the faces of his friends.

He sat back, gently drumming his fingers on the surface of his desk, his thoughts spinning wildly. He stayed where he was until he felt certain about what to do.

He picked up the phone and tapped a number.

"Lee, I want you in my office now."

Lee Marker was tall and lean, with a pale-eyed stare that could unnerve anyone he directed it to. He was Granger's closest ally and totally loyal when it came to carrying out his employer's orders.

"Close the door, Lee. Sit down. A serious problem has come up and we need some decisive action if we're going to come through it. I'm going to put you in the picture first. When I'm done we need a solution," Granger said.

Marker listened as Granger detailed everything, from the 1995 incident to the current situation. When Granger finished Marker was silent for a few seconds. Granger watched him closely, trying to fathom what was going through the man's mind.

"Lee?"

"I knew I did the right thing when I joined up with

you. I just never realized *how* right. Ramsey, you are one son of a bitch."

"I'll take that as a compliment. Now what do we do?"

"I know what I'd do. First get hold of that disk—"

"And destroy it?"

"Hell, no, boss. Keep it. We turn it against every mother in the consortium. Use it to keep them in line. Make them dance to your tune. How many times have I heard you say you're sick of the way they operate? Here's your chance. As soon as Thorne comes up with a location, we get our people into place. We take charge of the disk and back off. Secure the item in a safe place and call a meeting."

Marker sat back and waited. A thin smile edged Granger's lips. "Seems reasonable to me." He gave Marker a slight nod. "Do it, Lee. If there's collateral damage, well, these things happen."

Granger's confidence was shaken when he received the call from Billingham, informing him that Tira Malivic was dead and worse, the snatch team that had taken her friend, Erika Dukas, had been wiped out by a lone individual who had released her. Billingham said the pair had vanished.

Washington, D.C.

THE NEWS OF HIS NIECE'S DEATH stunned Pavlic. He sat in his hotel room and watched the news coverage, and knew that her death was his fault. There were mentions of a second body in the apartment and a live individual secured to a radiator. He was not sure what that meant. The Washington Police Department would make no further comment.

He sat for some time staring at the television screen after he had switched off, trying to make some kind of sense out of events. It seemed obvious that his flight from Sarajevo was the catalyst of the whole affair. His journey to Paris, then Washington, had been monitored, and somehow Radin's people had connected him to Tira. Radin would have informed Billingham, who could have easily arranged for the follow-up. Buy it off, or destroy it. Pavlic had seen the signs over the past months as close associates in the consortium had been removed as their usefulness waned, and it had been in that atmosphere of creeping unease that he had found his own existence becoming less secure…and another name came to mind.

Ramsey Granger.

The other American who had been with Billingham on that fateful day. If Billingham was powerful and dangerous, Granger was worse. Once he entered the equation—and Pavlic knew he would—the stakes would become even higher and Pavlic's life would be worth less than nothing. Pavlic knew Granger on a professional and personal basis. He had met the man on many trips to the U.S., and the one thing he had learned was that Ramsey Granger was dangerous.

Pavlic made a couple of calls to contacts back in Sarajevo. It didn't take long to get the answers he needed, and they verified his worst fears.

Hac Tivik was dead.

Pavlic's contact passed along more information. Radin, Jatko and his team had left the country. They'd taken Karel Medusku with them. And a Frenchman by the name of Dupré. Pavlic knew a computer expert Jatko used regularly. The man had extreme computing skills at his disposal.

Sev Malik, the remaining top executive in the consortium, had remained in Sarajevo to oversee matters while Radin was out of the country.

After completing his call Pavlic had paced his hotel suite, his mind troubled by what he had learned. He was in no doubt as to where Radin and company had gone. They were on their way to the U.S.A., and they would be looking for him as he searched for the package. His plan to get the incriminating disk out of Bosnia, as farsighted as it was, would amount to nothing if Radin and his people closed in.

He set up his laptop and connected to the Internet by the outlet provided in the room. He logged in to his server and went online, first running a quick check on his bank accounts. The first thing he saw was the warning message that an attempt had been made to access the accounts by an unauthorized user. His safeguard had worked—on the downside it confirmed that his deposits had been diskovered. That would be Dupré. Pavlic knew that the French expert would not quit. He knew his reputation and given enough time he would bypass even Pavlic's security protocols. It would be foolish to sit back and convince himself he was safe. He transferred a substantial cash amount from one of the accounts, placing it in a normal bank account that he could access via ATMs. He was going to need money for what he needed to do. Then he made some more transfers of the bulk of his hoard, placing the money in different accounts that he had prepared for such emergencies, setting up even more cryptic access codes that would delay Dupré even longer. His final act was to enable a powerful virus that would, on unauthorized access attempts to the original accounts, kick back with a destructive attack on Dupré's own computer.

His e-mail alert told him he had a message. Pavlic opened it and saw it was from his niece. The message was in Serbian. It was short and to the point:

Sent to the place I promised I would show you one day. In your name.

Pavlic understood immediately. It made him smile for an instant. He knew exactly what Tira had meant. He experienced regret that it would not happen now. She would never show him her favorite place in America. The place she loved to go when she had the time. That was gone, taken from her by the savagery of the men who were looking for him.

He deleted the e-mail, then called for the next flight to Colorado.

PAVLIC CHECKED OUT OF THE hotel an hour later, the cab he had ordered taking him directly to Dulles. His nonstop flight to Denver International departed at 7:00 p.m, weather permitting. The forecasts for the Denver area were warning of snow. Pavlic wasn't bothered about that. If he could get to his destination and locate the package, he would take the next step when it presented itself.

Compton Field, Virginia

"ARE YOU SURE THAT THING WILL get us to Colorado?"

The blunt question made Bolan smile. He was becoming used to her direct manner. He turned from his map. She was standing at the window of the control tower, looking down at the rain-swept apron where the Cessna Titan aircraft rocked slightly in the wind. The plane was fine as far as Bolan was concerned, but Dukas wasn't convinced.

"Would I lie to you?" he asked.

"If you thought it would calm me down, yes. You'd tell me that airplane out there is the safest thing ever built."

"You ask my buddy, Jack," Bud Casper said from the other side of the room. "He's flown her plenty of times." Casper was the pilot. A fair-haired, lean, good looking man in his thirties, he wore tan Chinos and a sweatshirt.

Jack Grimaldi had directed Bolan to the small local airstrip when the Executioner had requested help chartering a flight. Whatever Grimaldi had said to the pilot had worked. By the time Bolan and Dukas arrived at Compton Field the Cessna was fueled and ready to go.

Bolan was using his civilian cover name of Matt Cooper, and from the way Casper greeted him it was plain that Grimaldi had laid down the ground rules. The pilot asked no questions apart from their destination, and he and Bolan had spent some time poring over flight charts, leaving Dukas clutching a mug of coffee as she stared out the window, convincing herself that the plane was too flimsy to resist the rough weather.

"Are you sure those wings should move like that?"

Casper came to stand beside her.

"If they were too rigid, they'd snap off the minute we hit any turbulence."

"*Snap* and *turbulence* are not words I want to hear right now," Dukas said.

"Miss, trust me, I'm a pilot. Nothing's about to go wrong."

Dukas smiled wearily.

"We ready to go?" Bolan asked.

Casper and Dukas nodded.

On their way to Compton Field Bolan had stopped off to purchase new clothing and footwear for the trip. With snow country in mind Bolan had made certain they were prepared.

As they emerged from the tower, turning their backs to the rain, Casper ran ahead to open up the Cessna. Dukas followed, carrying one of the backpacks, and Bolan brought up the rear with rest of their gear.

Bolan saw Casper pause to look over his shoulder

and skyward as he picked up sound. The muffled noise of a chopper's rotors had filtered through Bolan's selective hearing too, and he followed Casper's lead, raising his head toward the source. It was coming in from the south, the unmistakable sound long imprinted on the Executioner's memory.

Dukas, becoming aware of their diverted attention, stopped and checked them both out.

"What is it?"

"Helicopter," Bolan said.

"And that means?"

Bolan's answer was to drop the pack he carried, crouching to open a zipper and reach inside. He pulled out an H&K MP-5, quickly checking the magazine and breech. He snapped back the cocking bolt, rising to his feet and waiting, the weapon held down and parallel with his right leg.

"Cooper?" Casper said.

"Load the gear, Bud," Bolan replied.

Casper grabbed the pack Bolan had dropped. He opened the passenger access hatch and shoved it inside, then took the one Dukas held.

"Go stand with Bud," Bolan said as he moved away from the Cessna, following the dark outline of the helicopter as it circled the field and angled in toward the waiting plane. As it lowered to ten feet off the ground, Bolan stepped clear of the Cessna. The chopper's pilot nursed the aircraft to follow him.

Bolan spotted the Bell-430 model. It was dark blue and white with no corporate logos, landing wheels locked down. He could make out figures in the passenger compartment behind the pilot.

"Both of you onboard. Bud, wind her up. Be ready to go when I give the word," Bolan shouted.

The chopper hovered a few feet aboveground, movement was clearly visible behind the cabin windows. The side hatch opened and a figure leaned out, making no attempt to conceal the autopistol he held.

"All we want is the woman," the man called above the sound of the rotors.

Bolan circled, bringing the chopper side on. Behind the guy in the hatchway he saw others crowding the cabin space, just waiting for the command.

Bolan caught the movement of legs dropping into sight on the opposite side of the aircraft. Someone was climbing out on the far side. The man dropped to the ground as Bolan brought the MP-5 into play. He raked the engine housing with a long burst, then hit the tail rotor. He saw fragments spin free. Smoke began to trail from the engine housing, whipped away by wind and the damaged tail rotor locked.

The pilot found he was losing stability and fought to compensate. The chopper rotated in the opposite direction to the main rotors. The sweeping body came around and hit the man who had exited the craft. He was sent headlong to the ground as the chopper sank to the ground.

It landed hard, jarring the occupants. The gunner in the hatchway opened fire on Bolan's moving figure, his shots scoring the concrete at the Executioner's feet.

Bolan turned, secured his position and returned fire, tracking the 9 mm slugs into the shooter. The man let go of his weapon and slumped back inside. The pilot fought hard to maintain some kind of stability despite time being against him. He was dealing in seconds, and they counted down too fast for him to react. The chopper made a clumsy attempt to right itself, then swung violently. Gunners were fighting one another as they struggled to climb from the open hatch.

One fell, landing hard, dragging another with him. This man landed lightly, pushing to his feet and made a dash in Bolan's direction. He hauled a squat handgun from a hip holster and started to track on the Executioner, but Bolan had already altered his position and fired first, stitching the guy hard from groin to ribs. The impacting slugs drove the man to his knees, his pistol bouncing from his grip as he struck the hard, rain-slick concrete.

Bolan ran for the Cessna. The propellors were already spinning. Dukas had the passenger door held open, and Bolan threw his weapon inside and scrambled after it.

"Go," he yelled and felt the Cessna vibrate as Casper released the brake and hit the throttles.

As the aircraft rolled away from the apron in the direction of the runway, Bolan leaned out the door and saw the chopper still turning, the bulk of the aircraft slowly arcing until a spinning rotor struck the concrete. The stricken helicopter seemed to fall apart as it was drawn into the powerful spin of the rotors, dragging its own carcass across the concrete, debris bursting free. Bolan hauled the door shut and locked the lever.

Turning, he saw Dukas half on one of the passenger seats, eyes wide and unblinking, watching him as if he were some alien creature.

"Is it always like this for you?" she asked. "I mean, do you ever have a quiet moment?"

Bolan shrugged. He checked the MP-5 and fed in a fresh magazine before he put the weapon aside.

The Cessna lifted off from the runway and made the wide turn that would put them on course for Colorado.

"So how did they find us so easily?" Dukas asked.

"My fault," he said. "That SUV we took must have had a GPS tracking unit built in. I should have thought of that. Means the vehicle gives off a location signal that relays back to a monitoring base."

"So they could just sit and watch our progress on a monitor?"

Bolan nodded. He was to blame, no one else. In the rush to get Dukas clear he hadn't considered the possibility. It was a simple error but one that had put them in danger.

"Hey, you had enough to handle. Including this wimp," Dukas joked.

"I need to talk to Bud," Bolan said.

"Well, I'm sure he"ll appreciate being warned about whatever attack might be coming up in the next ten minutes," Dukas said, straight-faced.

Bolan dropped into the copilot's seat and looked through the windshield. The aircraft's wipers were busy with the rain. Even though Casper had taken them to a high altitude, they had not risen above the storm.

"Radio reports say the weather's going to be worse the farther west we go. By the time we hit the Rockies, we're going to have bad snow," the pilot said.

"Anytime you figure flying is too risky, Bud, you put us down and we'll pick up some wheeled transport," Bolan replied.

"Nah, I don't quit on my passengers. Didn't Big Jack tell you that?"

"He said next to him you were one of the best."

"Hell, I must have upset that fly jockey. Time was, he'd tell you next to him I *was* the best. He getting grumpy in his old age?"

Bolan nodded.

"Something like that. Bud, I'm grateful for your help, and the lack of questions."

"No sweat. Jack told me you keep things close. I figure you'll tell if it's necessary. Hell, it's been worth it for the excitement. Makes a change from my normal charters."

The radio crackled and Casper made contact. It was Harry from Compton Field.

"Just who you got onboard there, Bonnie and Clyde? Hellsfire, Bud, I got a smoking chopper on the apron and those pantywaists who flew in her got picked up by a four-by-four and burned rubber when they quit."

"Cooper, here, is a government agent, Harry. This is one of those need-to-know things. Harry, you don't need to know," Casper said.

"Everybody's a comic these days," Harry grumbled. "You go easy."

Casper signed off. "Couple of big flasks of coffee back there," he said. "Appreciate a mug myself, Cooper."

Bolan stood up, laying a hand on Casper's shoulder.

"Thanks for everything, Bud. I'll go fetch that coffee."

Miami

"TWO DEAD. THREE INJURED. One helicopter wrecked," Billingham said. "Wasn't there something else? Oh yes—they fucking well got away. Flew off into the wild, blue, fucking yonder." There was silence over the radio link.

"Bronson, you still there? Oh, good, for a moment I thought maybe you'd gone to start a collection to pay for my helicopter," Billingham shouted.

"I'm here, sir."

"I want you on their trail as soon as you deal with the dead and injured. I have Dupré hacking into the computer system at that hayseed airstrip to find out what flight plan that Cessna's pilot logged. Get back here. We need to get to this woman. And this time we don't lose her."

He slammed down the phone, shaking his head in frustration. What the hell did it take to stop two men and a woman? Obviously an armed group in a helicopter wasn't the answer. If they had got the GPS tracking unit online sooner the chopper team might have arrived earlier. They had missed that chance. They would need to do better next time.

Billingham didn't notice Erik Dupré enter the cabin until the Frenchman spoke his name.

"What?" He turned, still in a rage.

Dupré held up a printout sheet. "This."

"What did you find out?" Billingham asked.

"The charter's destination is Maple Lake, Colorado, with a stop at Springfield-Branson in Missouri. For refueling, I'd guess," Dupré said.

"Maple Lake?"

"Some kind of vacation area in the mountains. Didn't mean much until I accessed Malivik's laptop your boys picked up at her apartment. She and this Dukas woman used to spend time up there at some lodge their families visited for years. She had an online diary with photographs of the place and the town close by."

"All very cozy," Billingham said. "Does it have anything to do with our package?"

"Yes. I checked out Malivik's plastic and found a payment for a special delivery parcel a few days ago. U.S. Postal Service to a collection drop in Maple Lake. To be picked up by a Mr. L. Pavlic."

"Damn," Billingham said. "Okay, we concentrate on Maple Lake. We need to get there fast."

"We can get a team assembled," Jatko said.

"Good. I'll arrange air transport and ground vehicles through Granger. Anything else I need to know?"

"Right now there's a snowstorm brewing out there," Dupré said.

Billingham smiled. "That should work fine for us." He stood up. "Time to organize, people."

Radin stared at him. "You're going too?"

"Damn right I am." He smiled wider. "Correction—we're all going."

RAMSEY GRANGER TOOK Billingham's call and listened as the details were passed along. He had been waiting for the call so he could move his own people. He informed Billingham that there would be equipment and transport waiting for him at a private airstrip in Colorado that would get them close to Maple Lake. Once he had completed the call he passed the information to Marker.

"They took their time getting it," Marker observed.

8

An hour into the flight, Bolan had taken a seat toward the rear of the cabin. Dukas was up front, her seat tilted back as she slept. Bolan had found a blanket in the overhead locker and had draped it over her. Now he took the opportunity to relax, though his mind was still active as he went over the events leading up to this flight. He was also wondering what lay ahead in Colorado.

Complete identification of the shadowy figures behind the recent events had yet to be verified. They had names but little else at the moment. The only sure thing Bolan knew was the deadly intent of the people involved. Exhibiting a ruthless determination to claim the package, they had left Tira Malivik dead and then had pursued Erika Dukas with the same disregard for her life.

Bolan's curiosity was directed toward the contents of that package. He reasoned that to have brought about such violence they had to be explosive. He realized there was nothing to gain in such speculation at this point. The enemy had drawn the line, their actions marking them as savage in their pursuit. Erika

Dukas was just a pawn in their deadly game. That fact alone had been enough to draw Bolan into the arena. The intense hunt would go on until the prize had been claimed. Bolan had no intention of allowing it go to the opposition. The harder they pushed the harder he would resist.

They hadn't realized that yet.

In his current mood Bolan had no intention of cutting them any slack.

THEY MADE A REFUELING STOP at the Springfield-Branson Regional Airport in Missouri. The weather had deteriorated, as Casper had predicted. It was starting to snow as they took off again. While the refueling took place, Casper crossed to the terminal building and came back with food and the flasks refilled with coffee. Dukas woke when they touched down, took time to eat and went back to sleep once they were in the air. Bolan took his place beside Casper.

"I meant what I said, Bud," Bolan reminded him. "No risk clause is included in your contract."

Casper only grinned.

"Hey, I paid my dues back in the Gulf War, then Afghanistan. AH-64 Apache attack helicopters. Like I said before, Coop, a little action is welcome. This charter stuff is okay, but man, it gets dull."

"You didn't want to stay in the service?"

"Nah. Wasn't for me. I'm not disciplined enough. So I figured I'd try the quiet life. I just didn't realize how quiet it was going to turn out." He grinned at

Bolan. "Back there at Compton it felt like I was in the damn war again."

Bolan didn't reply. He waited until Casper spoke again. "Yeah, okay, I miss the action."

Increasingly heavy snow lashed out of the leaden sky, the flakes thick and heavy. Casper was depending on his radar to keep him on course. If he was concerned, he didn't show it. He was a more than competent pilot, handling the bad weather with calm assurance. Bolan left him to it after a time. He returned to the passenger cabin and resumed his seat, relaxing as much as he could. He knew he should get some rest while the opportunity presented itself. There might not be much on offer once they reached Colorado. The opposition was going to be close by, he was sure. After everything that had already happened, they weren't about to quit. It was the only thing they all had in common.

THE EXECUTIONER OPENED HIS EYES as the Cessna began to vibrate around him. He took a moment to clear his head before pushing to his feet, reaching out to brace himself against the sway of the cabin floor. As he made his way forward, he saw Dukas was rousing herself.

"What's wrong?" she asked.

"Just on my way to find out."

Dukas glanced out of the cabin window and was shocked to see the sky thick with swirling, heavy snow. She stood and hurried forward, seeing Bolan's tall figure hovering behind the pilot's seat.

"Hey, have you seen what it's like out there?" she asked.

If Bolan heard he made no reply.

She heard Bud Casper's calm voice. "Coop, you want the good news, or the bad news?"

"I'll bite."

"Bad news is there ain't no good news," Casper said grimly.

Bolan leaned over the copilot's seat. There was little to see beyond the windshield. The wipers were struggling to keep the screens clear.

"Weather has gone ballistic—and I mean *ballistic*."

"How bad is that?" Dukas asked.

Bolan was checking the instrument array. "Bud, are we off course?"

"Some. I keep losing the radar signal. I guess we've drifted off our flight path. Been trying to pull her back, but the controls are getting sluggish. Build up of the snow and one hell of a temperature drop. And that wind out there is way up the scale. Hate to say it, folks, but we caught all the bad luck in one throw."

"Any good news?" Dukas asked.

"Coffee is still hot."

"Bud, where were we last time you had a solid fix?" Bolan asked.

"I was getting ready to lose height for landing approach. Lost communication before I got through to the field. Didn't have time to do anything because she started pitching and rolling. One of the problems in this mountain region is you get weird changes in air currents. Especially in bad weather. That was about when we started to lose line of flight."

The Cessna dropped suddenly as they encountered another air pocket, and Casper fought the controls. "Day keeps getting better and better," he muttered.

Bolan picked up an uneven beat coming from the starboard engine. He saw that Casper had noticed too. The pilot glanced through the side screen, his hand moving to the engine controls, and he started to work them. The irregular pulse of the engine settled for a moment, then returned.

"We're losing her," was all he said. *"Damn."*

"I have a feeling we're not going to make the Maple Lake strip," Dukas said.

"You have to state the obvious?" Casper replied.

The starboard engine died, made an attempt to power up again but choked and the propellor stalled. Casper made immediate adjustments to compensate, but not before the Cessna swooped and tilted. "All we need is a whiteout to make the day perfect."

"Could that happen now?" Dukas asked.

"If it does and we're still in the air, you'll know," Casper said. "I'm going to look for a soft landing spot and try to bring her down. And I need to do it soon."

"Do it then," Bolan said.

He turned to Dukas. "Go and strap yourself in tight."

She made no argument as she turned away.

Bolan dropped into the seat next to Casper. He locked his own seat belt, then donned the copilot's headset and started to put out a distress call.

The Cessna lost height rapidly, cleaving its way through the wind-driven swirls of snow. Casper hauled back on the controls as he struggled to maintain a stable descent. Working with a single engine did little to help the situation. He had made a couple passes over his chosen landing site, having assessed the possibility of the long, open strip between opposing peaks. It was the best he was going to be offered. The snow and ice buildup on the wings and control surfaces had increased, and keeping the Cessna in the air was becoming harder. He decided that attempting a risky landing was preferable to crashing. Once he had made his decision he went for it without further delay.

Beside him, Bolan was still putting out calls. He had received no response. He understood the problems. The bad weather conditions and the surrounding high peaks could have been affecting the transmissions. Dead spots occurred in these mountainous regions. Taken together the problems added up to nothing encouraging.

He felt the Cessna drop again, heard Casper mutter something vaguely obscene. The pilot made swift, sure adjustments to hand and foot controls, pulling the reluctant aircraft back on course for the mist-shrouded landing space ahead. It was coming up fast, very fast, and even Bolan found the sight disturbing. There was a feeling about this kind of situation that stayed out of reach, leaving him totally unable to intervene. He was a spectator, facing a possible disaster, a voyeur held by the spectacle, beyond being part of it, simply waiting.

The landing wheels hit. The Cessna bounced back

into the air, the airframe vibrating wildly. Casper juggled the controls and brought the plane down again, this time keeping it there. The vibration began again, the ripples sweeping back and forth, blinding clouds of disturbed snow obscuring their surroundings. The howl of the engine rose, and Bolan felt himself pushed against his seat belt as the Cessna fought gravity and its own forward motion. Their speed dropped surprisingly swiftly, the heavy vibration lessening as well, and the forward rush became a steady roll, then a swaying halt.

Bolan let go of held breath as the Cessna came to a full stop. He hadn't realized just how tense he was. Sinking back in his seat he glanced across at Casper. "Hell of a job there, Bud."

Casper didn't speak until he had cut the engines and shut down the power. He cleared his own throat. "We hope you enjoyed your flight and don't forget us for your return trip."

"No problem with the last part," Dukas said from behind them. "This is one flight I will never ever forget."

Casper twisted in his seat.

"You okay?"

"I'm fine, Bud. A little shaky but fine."

"We all ready for a hike?" Bolan said.

"Does this guy ever give up?" Casper inquired.

Dukas shook her head. "What do you think?"

9

Colorado

A couple of times Lec Pavlic had felt the powerful four-by-four slide and he had almost lost control. He forced himself to slow down. The road from Denver, though almost empty of traffic, was hard to judge. He was not used to the huge vehicle and its power, and despite his need to get to Maple Lake he forced himself to take more care. His chance of survival was going to fall to zero if he found himself in a roadside ditch, or worse, careering down one of the steep slopes he was seeing as he drove higher into the mountains.

He had been driving for almost three hours, leaving the main highways behind for a narrower road that wound its way into the craggy heights in a series of sweeping curves.

According to his GPS route finder he was still on the right road, moving closer, though slowly, to Maple Lake. The young woman at the car rental agency had keyed in the required coordinates for him and had run through the way to read the display.

Through the falling snow he spotted the lights of a diner and gas station. He decided to take a break. The strain of driving the winding slopes was getting to him. Some food and coffee would help, and he decided that it would also be wise to top up the gas tank. The last thing he needed was to run out of fuel.

He drew up at the pumps and climbed out as the attendant came from the office.

"Hell of a day," the young man said. "Fill her up?"

"To the top, please."

The attendant zipped up his thick jacket, turning up the collar and yanking down the long bill of his cap. He started to fill the tank. "Where you heading?"

"Maple Lake. You know it?"

"Yeah. You got business there?"

"Oh, yes. I'm checking out some property for my investment company. They're looking to put some money into the town. I hear it's a nice summer vacation spot," Pavlic said.

The attendant smiled and checked the sky.

"Ain't exactly summer right now, mister."

"I was in the country on other business and head office said to check out the place. They pay my salary, so I do what I'm told. This time I will just be looking the place over."

They made small talk until, the refueling complete, Pavlic followed the young man into the office. He paid for the gas and gave a generous tip.

"Hey, thanks. You take care on those roads. The weather forecast isn't too good." He grinned suddenly.

"If this keeps up, you might get stuck in Maple Lake *until* the summer. At least then you'll see just how nice it is."

"Good thought," Pavlic said. He indicated the diner's parking lot. "I'm going to park over there and get some coffee and food before I drive on."

As he left the SUV and tramped through the snow to the diner and its welcome warmth, the young man's words kept running through his mind.

You might get stuck in Maple Lake.

That very thought had been in his head for a while. If he ran into Billingham and company he might very well get stuck in Maple Lake—*permanently.*

"THEY'RE DOWN," ERIC DUPRÉ announced. He swiveled his laptop and pointed out the salient points of the display. "They missed the landing site by a wide margin."

"Of course," Billingham said.

"Just as you suggested," Radin said. "So what do we do now?"

"We find them," Jatko said. "It's why we came here. To prevent them getting their hands on the disk and finding out what's on it."

"Have you noticed the weather out there? It's the reason they've ended up off course. This isn't going to be a walk in the park," Radin said.

"Milos, we are on the ground. Our team is equipped with the best money can buy." Billingham gestured at the cargo, including a couple of civilian Humvees, stowed in the belly of the C-130 Hercules that had brought them to Colorado and the internal freight division where the plane was now parked next to a cargo warehouse. "They are well armed, every man carrying a satellite GPS unit. They're tied into Dupré's computer system so they won't get lost. He already has that downed plane on-screen. We send out our team and they can run a wide sweep over the area. I don't believe it will be hard to find our quarry. They'll be heading for Maple Lake."

"The team is ready to go," Jatko said. "You want to talk with them first?"

Billingham made his way along the cargo bay and confronted his hired team. Led by Jatko, who had his own men—Milic and Anton—along as well, the group was clad in all-weather clothing and carried the best equipment money could buy. In addition to the GPS units, they were all equipped with digital transceivers that would enable them to stay in contact with one another and Billingham's command base.

"You all know why you're here. Simple enough. The people we're after are attempting to get their hands on something belonging to the company. That has to be prevented. Kill the two men, but I want the woman alive. You all know me. I pay well for your expertise. That also demands total loyalty. I think you know what I'm talking about. If the package falls into anyone's hands, it is to be brought directly to me. Do not even entertain the thought of making a personal deal for the package. Do your job, accept your pay and we can do business again in the future. Do we understand each other?"

Jatko nodded. "They understand."

"One more thing. Mr. Jatko will pass out copies of a photograph. There's a chance that the man shown there might turn up. I want this man dead. He is a threat to all our livelihoods. He is out to damage the company. Under no circumstances is he to be allowed to interfere with our business. See him—kill him. This is not negotiable. I will pay a high bonus to see him on the ground with his brains next to him."

Jatko stepped forward to give his final instructions.

"Make sure your GPS and transceivers are online. As soon as that's done, move out. Dupré will keep you informed of the location of that Cessna. Find it and the people on it. Keep all weapons out of sight until you're off-road. No point in attracting attention."

Radin followed Billingham and Jatko back along the plane. They walked down the loading ramp and, heads bowed against the wind-driven snow, made their way into the storage hangar they were using. In one corner was a block of offices, Karel Medusku sat on a hard chair, silent, deep in a mood of his own making.

"Was it necessary to say that?" Radin asked Billingham as they entered the office. Behind them Jatko quietly closed the door, leaning against it, staring across at Medusku's hunched figure.

"About double-crossing us? Of course. They already know I do not play games. I was simply reinforcing the matter. Paid help sometimes need reminding who the paymaster is."

"I was thinking more about Pavlic. If he does show

his face and realizes he has no chance at getting hold of the disk he might decide to talk. Even though it might condemn him too," Radin said.

"I worked that out myself, which is exactly why I gave those instructions. The last thing we need is Pavlic making a final grand gesture. I won't take the chance of him turning up and spilling his guts on national television. I've been thinking what he might do since he vanished from Washington. He's on his way to Maple Lake. I know it. So if he does show his face he will get it shot off."

Medusko looked up. He was pale. Graying stubble covered his jaw. "This is not going to get us anywhere," he said.

"Ah, it still talks," Jatko said. "Do you have something constructive to say?"

Medusku stood up, confronting Jatko.

"You believe you are smart. But none of you were smart enough to stop Pavlic from leaving the country and flying to America. Not smart enough to prevent him moving the package to a safe location. One man has fooled us all. Doesn't it make you think he might stay one step ahead and expose us all?"

"Look at the men and equipment we have assembled, Karel," Radin said. "I think *we* have the advantage now."

"It won't work. We thought we had the perfect solution ten years ago. It has caught up with us. You know what? I think we were wrong then, and we are wrong now."

Jatko's laugh held a mocking tone. "*Wrong?* Wrong to protect ourselves?"

"Suddenly *we* are the victims?" Medusku asked. "The people we murdered were the victims. We killed them and sold our souls for profit and power."

"No," Jatko shouted. "Those mongrels were the enemy."

"You seem to have forgotten we were at war back then," Radin said.

"Are you going to say what we did was an *act of war?* Or simply an excuse for slaughter?"

"Conflict has the effect of creating situations that call for decisive action," Radin said.

Medusku shook his head. "So I comfort myself by believing those six people were our *enemy?*"

"Weren't they? Just recall who they were. From the opposing side. All we were doing was gaining an advantage over the enemy side. The definition of armed conflict," Radin replied.

"Oh, I see. And the money? The political maneuvering? That had nothing to do with it?"

Radin's face stiffened, color flaring in his cheeks.

"I didn't think even you could be so naive, Karel. It became necessary for our survival. It is what happens during war. The need to survive is an instinct as natural as breathing. Take those instincts away, and how long would we stay alive?"

"We had no choice, Karel," Billingham said. He had been standing back, listening to the ongoing argument. His intervention was an attempt at calming the moment down. "No choice."

Medusku forced at bitter smile. "Ah, the oldest excuse in the book. *We had no choice.* You are wrong, Thorne. We *always* have a choice."

"Yes," Radin said, "and we made ours. Even you, Karel. I don't have any recollection of you objecting at the time. Or during the decade since."

"You are right, Milos. I'm as guilty as you all. I have blood on my hands. The problem is, I see it every time I close my eyes. I hate what we have become. Look at us now. One young woman dead and another being pursued across America. For what? Just how many do we have to kill to keep our secret?"

Jatko's pent-up anger burst to the surface. He lunged at Medusku and caught hold of him by his coat. He swung the man around and smashed him against the wall.

"As many as it takes," he screamed. "You think I care how many? Or who they are? Watch and see."

"Your answer to everything, eh, Maric. If it doesn't suit you, eliminate it," Medusku said.

"Exactly. So if I was you I would choose my words carefully from now on."

Medusku smiled wearily. "You don't frighten me any longer, Maric. There's nothing you can threaten me with that I haven't already accepted."

"Maybe I will put you out of your misery soon then."

Medusku simply shrugged. He returned to his seat.

They turned and left the office, heading through

the warehouse. Midway Jatko stopped in midstride, his face set and pale. He remained where he was, waging an inner struggle that seemed to be consuming him.

"Maric?" Billingham asked as he realized Jatko had fallen behind.

Radin looked back at Jatko and realized what was happening immediately. He held Jatko's unblinking stare. "You are sure?" he asked.

Jatko nodded sharply. He reached inside his coat and drew out his 9 mm Glock. He worked the slide, turned on his heel and retraced his steps to the office.

"Milos?" Billingham said.

Radin reached out to place a hand on Billingham's arm. He turned him, guiding him toward the exit. They had just stepped outside when the twin cracks of a 9 mm pistol sounded. They stopped, but only Billingham looked back to see Jatko stepping out of the office and crossing the warehouse to join them again.

"Dilemmas need to be resolved," Radin said. "We were all aware Medusku was on the edge. Right from the start. Remember how he pushed Pavlic into running. He could easily have betrayed us too because of his own doubts. We should be grateful Maric had the courage to do what we all wanted but failed to carry out."

It did make sense, Billingham realized. It also convinced him to keep any doubts he might have to himself, and not to air them in the presence of Maric Jatko.

Billingham waved a finger at him.

"Which is why we are here. To put this mess in order. I have too much going for me to back down because of Pavlic."

Jatko nodded in agreement.

"Milos, have faith. We handled Tivik and the Malivik woman. We're close to finding Dukas and the location of the disk. Be patient."

10

They made final a attempt to contact Maple Lake. The radio emitted only muffled static. Casper switched off. "So much for modern technology."

They had donned their backpacks, Bolan carrying his MP-5 in his hand, the Beretta 93-R in his shoulder rig under his parka. Dukas still had the pistol Bolan had given her and Casper had a 9 mm Browning in a hip holster. They wore caps and thermal gloves.

"We set?" Bolan asked.

"You believe those people might show up?" Casper asked.

"They've done it so far. It isn't beyond their capabilities to work out where we were heading. Sooner or later this has to come together."

"Okay."

"Bud, you lead. Head toward Maple Lake," Bolan said.

"Erika, I want you between me and Bud. Keep close everybody. It's easy to get separated in this weather."

Dukas nodded, turning as Casper opened the hatch

and the chill wind blew into the cabin. They moved out of the Cessna, Casper closing the hatch and securing it.

They strung out in the formation Bolan had ordered, heads down against the stinging wind and snow. Visibility was poor, and it was apparent that Bolan had made the correct assumption. It wouldn't take much to get lost if any of them stepped away from the collective line of travel. Casper checked his position, indicated which way they needed to go and led the way. The dark outline of the Cessna quickly vanished as they crossed the open clearing, heading for the line of timber ahead.

Bolan kept his focus on Dukas as well as the surrounding terrain. His regard for her rose higher. Despite the trauma of the last day or so she was staying with the game. As she trudged through the thick carpet of snow, shoulders hunched against the slap of the wind, she made no protest. Her friendship with Tira Malivik had thrown her to the wolves, and had placed her in the position of having to take a life in order to survive. And she was coming through it. Taking whatever the situation threw at her. Bolan knew that took a special kind of courage—and it appeared that Erika Dukas had it within her. Bolan had accepted responsibility for her and in his book that carried an unspoken bond to see this through to a conclusion.

They walked for more than two hours, Casper's natural instincts allowing him to guide them with confidence. The pilot had that built-in homing ability that Bolan had seen in Jack Grimaldi on more than one occasion. In the air, or on the ground, the pilots developed a strong sense of direction that took them wherever they wanted to go with unerring accuracy. If the severe weather and mechanical failure hadn't forced Casper to make an emergency landing, Bolan was confident he would have put them down on the airstrip they had been heading for. But nature had a way of changing drastically, without prior warning, and putting up barriers that negated planned intentions. When that happened the only course was to roll with those changes and move on.

BOLAN NOTICED CONDITIONS WERE changing and called a halt. He led Dukas and Casper to the comparative shelter of some trees. Dukas leaned in close and asked what was wrong, her voice faint against the buffeting wind.

"More snow coming," Bolan said. He raised a hand and indicated the swirling cloud of white moving in from the higher slopes. "It's heading our way."

"If that hits before we get to Maple lake, or any kind of cover, we could really be in for trouble," Casper said.

"Is that your whiteout?" Dukas asked.

"It's brewing up for one."

She stared at Bolan. "Mr. Cooper, you really pull out all the stops for a first date."

"What can I say."

Bolan was about to move them out when he saw a dancing red spot on the front of Casper's coat. For a split second he couldn't believe it.

A laser dot. Somebody had them in his sights.

"Back," Bolan shouted, bringing up the MP-5.

The stuttering crackle of autofire added to his warning. Slugs chewed at tree bark, showering them with debris. Bolan planted a hand flat between the young woman's shoulders and shoved hard. Her strangled cry was lost as she fell facedown in the thick snow. A second volley followed, the line of slugs kicking up snow as it closed on Bolan and Casper. It was the pilot who moved a fraction too slowly. He caught a slug in his left thigh and he stumbled, slamming against a thick tree trunk. As he made to pull himself around, more slugs thudded into the trunk. One hammered into his left shoulder, spraying a bloody mist as Casper slid around the tree and pitched into the snow.

Bolan dropped to a crouch. As his eyes picked up the shooter moving forward from deep snow cover, swinging his weapon for another burst, Bolan brought up the MP-5 and locked on his target. He held his shot until he was sure, then stroked the trigger and fired a short burst.

The instant he fired Bolan adjusted his aim slightly and fired once more. The first burst hit the man in the throat, the follow-up cored into his chest. The shooter went flat on his back, arms wide, eyes open and staring up at the snow-laden sky.

Dukas was on her knees beside Casper.

"Do what you can. I'll be back," Bolan said, turning away and running to where the downed shooter lay. The discarded weapon lay in the snow beside him, an

M-16 A-3 with a laser sight mounted on a picatinny rail. Bolan crouched beside the still form. He found a Glock 17 and tucked it in his belt. He checked the man's pockets and found some extra clips for the handgun and more for the M-16 in belt pouches. He saw the GPS unit the man had been carrying from a neck strap. One of Bolan's slugs had plowed directly into the unit, shattering the casing and destroying the tracking capabilities. There was a transceiver clipped to the man's belt. Bolan took it and pushed it into a pocket. Then he picked up the M-16 and slung it from his shoulder.

He returned to where Dukas had opened her backpack, dragging out a shirt. He handed her a lock knife from his pocket and she sliced the material into strips. With Bolan's help she wadded cloth over Casper's wounds, then tied them in place with longer strips.

"This isn't going to help long-term," she said. "He's going to need medical attention."

"*He* is listening," Casper said. He glanced at Bolan. "These jerks chasing you are getting to be a pain."

Dukas forced a smile.

"Welcome to our little club," she said. "Cooper and I have been banging heads with them longer than I've cared to."

Casper tensed as pain surged and engulfed his shoulder and leg. He bit down on the pain, unable to speak until the spasm ebbed away.

"We need to get him under cover," Dukas said. "He needs warmth and somewhere to rest."

Bolan was fully aware what was needed. Casper's wounds were not going to respond outside. Warmth and rest would help, Bolan knew, but on the mountain slopes that kind of thing lay beyond even Bolan's capabilities.

"How far to Maple Lake?" he asked Dukas.

"A long way in these conditions and on foot."

"You see any alternatives?"

"Give me a minute."

She checked their position, scanning the slopes for landmarks. It wasn't easy with the heavy snow. She walked around until she was satisfied.

"Don't hold me to this, but I'm pretty sure we're about four miles northwest of a local spot called Tyler's Peak." She indicated the direction. "That way. If I haven't misread, we should be less than two miles from a relief station. It's a cabin the town had built a few years back after people got lost in weather like this. It's maintained by the town council. I wouldn't expect to find anyone there, but they keep the places stocked with survival equipment. There might even be a radio."

Bolan glanced at Casper.

"If we can locate this cabin it should give us a chance."

"So why am I still lying here?" Casper asked.

Handing Dukas the MP-5, Bolan helped Casper to his feet. The injured pilot swayed a little, then accepted Bolan's supporting arm. They moved off slowly, setting a pace Casper could maintain without too much diskomfort. The thick snow underfoot slowed them even more.

Dukas took the lead. She tested the way ahead for

any hidden pitfalls beneath the blanket of fallen snow. Watching her, Bolan was impressed by her newly developed confidence. She was a determined survivor.

"You think there are any more close by?" Casper asked.

"Hard to say. I didn't see anyone with that guy. He may have separated from the others. Or maybe they're spreading themselves wide to up their percentage. Looks like his team is equipped with GPS units. Makes it easier for them to plan their way around."

"Good to know," Casper said.

Bolan checked out the high slopes.

"If that whiteout hits, even GPS units aren't going to be much help."

"I'm not about to hold my breath on that," Casper said.

Bolan agreed. There had to be more out there.

They made reasonable progress despite having to stop occasionally to allow Casper to rest. He wanted to keep moving, but Dukas was insistent that he take time out.

"She always this bossy?" Casper asked.

Bolan nodded.

Dukas ignored them.

"I think she likes us really," the pilot said.

Bolan had eased the man down so he could rest against a slab of rock. He checked Casper's wounds, using more of the torn shirt to make pressure pads to reduce blood loss.

"We still on track?" Bolan asked Dukas.

She indicated the distant rock formation she had called Tyler's Peak.

"As long as we keep that cleft as our central point, we're fine." She took a long look at the sky. "Just under an hour and we start to lose light. It gets dark quickly up here too."

"And cold," Bolan said. "Let's move on."

Bolan sensed a change in the wind. He threw a quick glance in the direction of the high peaks he had checked earlier. What he saw confirmed his suspicions.

The whiteout was heading their way. The seemingly solid fog of snow sweeping down off the slopes was closing on their position. If it hit before they reached cover, they would be overwhelmed, lost in a blinding cloud of all-encompassing snow. Direction would be meaningless, their senses nullified, and if they survived the extremes of snow, the freeze that often followed would stop them.

The snowfall thickened, reducing visibility and hampering their progress as it was pushed about by the eddying wind coming off the high peaks. It clung to their clothing and chilled their exposed faces. Casper stumbled a number of times, his deadweight falling against Bolan. Each time it happened, he apologized profusely. "Damn it, Coop, sorry."

"No problem."

"I feel like a useless idiot. Slowing you down and all. You'd have a better chance without me."

Dukas, close to Bolan's side, overheard the remark. "Don't you dare say that, Bud. Maybe those people chasing us could do that to one of their own. We don't."

"Well, I consider myself told," he said.

Bolan adjusted his grip on the wounded pilot as they moved on. "I warned you how she gets," he said.

"So you did."

The light faded quickly, shadows sweeping across the snow-covered slopes. Bolan found it harder to keep the distant marker they were homing on in clear sight.

Casper was becoming weaker. He struggled to stay awake, but finally even his resolve was exhausted and he passed out. Bolan caught him before he fell, lowering the unconscious pilot to the ground.

"Erika."

She turned back at his call. "What is it?"

"Bud passed out." Bolan was checking the bandages. They were sodden with the blood that had leaked through the material.

"Will he be all right?"

"If we can reach cover we can do something. Out here the only thing we have in plentiful supply is snow and cold."

"We should be close now," she said. Her face was showing signs of her own exhaustion. Bolan reached out and grasped her shoulder, shaking her none too gently.

"You can rest later," he said. "Right now we keep moving. Let's do it."

He deliberately used a harsh tone. The need to stay on their feet was the only thing that mattered right now. If they allowed their fatigue to dictate their actions, it would have been too easy to simply lie down and sleep. It was the insidious way that the cold played tricks with the mind, suggesting that they give up and let themselves slip into the soft embrace of exhaustion. From that it was a short step to a comatose state and a frozen death. The drop in temperature affected mobility and the ability to think coherently. They had to ignore the demands of the mind and force themselves to move on.

Bolan hauled Casper upright and hoisted him over his left shoulder. He paused for a moment to get his balance, then reached out with his free hand and pushed Dukas into motion.

"Now find that damned cabin," he growled.

Dukas pushed forward, her anger rising at his demands, and she hunched her shoulders against the bite of the wind.

"Just you watch," she shouted. "I'll find your cabin. Just you watch."

Behind her Bolan nodded at the anger in her words. His challenge got the response he wanted. She was mad enough now to walk clear across the Rockies without stopping.

11

Half buried by the drifting snow, the cabin might have been missed by someone not familiar with the local topography.

When Dukas finally recognized the location, she could have wept if she hadn't been so tired. She tramped through the thick snow and reached the solid wooden door, hoping the cabin hadn't been secured. She leaned against the door and worked the metal latch. It gave easily. She shoved hard and the door opened. Turning, she raised a hand to beckon Bolan. Her face registered sudden alarm, and Bolan threw a glance behind.

A wall of dense snow was sweeping in toward them. For a second Bolan was held immobile at the sight.

It was the whiteout, moving in on their position with an inexorable swiftness, tumbling mists of lighter snow preceding the solid bulk. He could feel the pressure pushing ahead of it, felt the threatening mass tumbling over the landscape and obliterating all in its path.

"Inside," he shouted above the harsh sound. "Just get inside."

He was already close behind, and she moved aside so he could step in. She turned, slamming the door and securing it with the internal bolts. As the final one slid into place she felt the solid thump as the rush of snow struck and swept over the cabin in its headlong sweep. The structure of the cabin shook. A dusting of snow filtered down through fine cracks in the roof beams.

From previous visits, she knew there were oil lamps stored on wall hooks. She made her way across the near-dark interior and found the lamps. On a small shelf above the lamps was a tin box that held matches. She took one out and struck it, lighting the lamp and turning it up the moment it flared.

There was a bank of wooden bunks against the rear wall. Bolan carried Casper over and placed him on one of the lower bunks. He immediately began to expose the man's wounds. Dukas took the lamp and set it down close by.

"I'll find the emergency kit," she said.

Bolan was removing Casper's bandages. Dukas lit a second lamp. then found the first-aid kit. Kneeling beside the bunk she opened the kit and let Bolan take what he wanted. From the way he operated it was obvious he had done this kind of thing before, so she removed herself and went to check the wood-burning stove. There was chopped wood in a box next to the stove. She located some splintered shreds she was able to use for kindling and got the stove lit. She fed in wood gradually until the stove started to give off heat. The warmth, as slight as it was initially, felt so good she would have stayed where she was if the situation hadn't been so desperate. As the hot air rose up the chimney, she heard the hiss of snow melting off the exposed peak.

She searched the supplies and found cans of food in a sealed carton.

"How is he?" she asked.

Bolan pulled a couple of blankets across Casper.

"As well as he's going to be until we can get him to a hospital."

He used an antiseptic wipe to clean his hands, and Dukas saw how slow his movements were.

"My turn to give the orders now," she said. "You go sit by the stove. I've got soup heating."

"Anytime I get stuck in a snowstorm I hope you're around, Erika Dukas. You make one hell of a guide."

She held his gaze, long enough to make her blush. Casper began groaning loudly enough to break the impasse. Bolan turned to check his patient.

Dukas returned to the stove and checked the soup while Bolan watched, resting while he had the chance.

Beyond the walls of the cabin they could still hear the howling wind. The cabin was solid, able to withstand the battering. Though neither spoke, both were wondering how long they might be forced to stay.

They consumed the hot soup with relish. There were soda crackers in another carton, and they ate them as well with enthusiasm. Even Casper managed a few mouthfuls before he drifted back into a restless sleep.

The sound of the strong winds outside reminded

them of their position and finally brought them to reality. Bolan eased open one of the window shutters and took a look. It was barely possible to see more than a few feet through the blinding white swirl of snow. Bolan secured the shutter again.

"Nothing we can do until morning," he said. "Did you say there might be some communications equipment?"

"I've already had a look. Nothing," Dukas said.

Bolan took out the transceiver he had taken from the man he'd shot. He examined the item.

"Can you call on that?" Dukas asked.

"I can change the frequency and send. Depends if anyone's listening on the other end."

"What about *them?*"

"Once I change the setting they won't pick up. All their sets will be on the same frequency so they're able to communicate."

"Hey, I forgot something." Dukas went to one of the cupboards. She opened a door and jabbed a finger at a printed notice taped to the panel. "Emergency numbers. I'm an idiot. There are numbers here to contact the sheriff's department in Maple Lake."

Bolan checked out the text. It listed telephone numbers and radio frequency settings. He set the transceiver to the recommended frequency and keyed the receive button. All he heard was a low static hiss. Bolan checked the transceiver's power level. It was high. He tried again. Nothing.

"We'll try again later," he said as he switched off the unit to conserve power.

"So what do we do now?"

"Keep warm and try to rest. Right now we're not going anywhere."

Bolan reached for his weapons and spent some time checking and making sure they were all fully loaded.

"Seeing you do that brings it home what we're doing here. I almost forgot about those men out there hunting for us." Tears filled her eyes and she wiped them away with an angry gesture. "I told myself I wasn't going to let this happen again. Then I remembered how I used to come up here with Tira. We swam in the lake. Rode all over the mountain—"

"Just hang on to those memories, Erika. Do that and you'll have your friend. Do her that favor and she'll always be with you."

They stoked the fire, dragged out all the blankets they could find and settled for the night. Despite her protests, Dukas finally took one of the bunks. She was asleep in minutes. Bolan checked Casper. The pilot seemed to have settled and at least his wounds had stopped bleeding. Bolan dragged a mattress off one of the empty bunks and dropped it against the back wall of the cabin. He took his MP-5 and sat on the mattress with a blanket around his shoulders, facing the door.

He took out the transceiver and ran through the channels again. There was nothing except the hiss of static. He switched it off again and placed it beside him.

He felt weariness wash over him. His eyes were drooping and he knew he was not going to be able to stay awake through the night. Too much had happened in a short span of time. He seemed to have been on the move ever since he had taken that call from Barbara Price, telling him one of their own had problems and needed help.

BOLAN WOKE WITH A START and stared around the cabin. Then he glanced at his watch and realized he had slept most of the night.

The stove was still warm. The lamps lit against the shadows. Bolan glanced across the open room. Dukas and Casper were still sleeping. He eased to his feet, working the stiffness from his body, turning to feed some wood into the stove, coaxing the red embers into flame.

Sound reached him from overhead and he picked up the hiss of frozen snow being blown across the cabin's slant roof. The noise told him there had been a partial freeze during the night. The soft snow had hardened into crystals. Bolan opened a shutter. It was not fully light, but he could see that the overpowering whiteout had expended its fury. There was only a light fall now. The constant wind was shifting the snow, blowing it back and forth over the landscape. That would make travel somewhat easier for them.

And for the men who had been trailing them the day before, he thought. Bolan closed the shutter.

He checked out the supply cupboard and found a metal coffeepot and a supply of ground coffee in a sealed tin. He smiled as he took them to the table. This was real cowboy country. He crossed to unbolt the door, opening it so he could scoop handfuls of snow into the pot. He secured the door and placed the pot on the stove.

The aroma of the coffee roused Casper. He groaned at a stab of pain when he moved, then remembered what had happened to him and lay still.

"Hey, Coop, how we doing?" he asked. His voice was low, weak, and he held no illusions as to his condition.

Bolan filled a mug and carried it across. He helped the pilot sit up.

Casper tasted the coffee and the grounds that had escaped the pot. "Great, coffee and breakfast in the same cup. Coop, you should patent this."

Bolan took a mug to Dukas and gently shook her awake. When her eyes opened, she stared up at him until her memory kicked in.

"I was somewhere else," she said. "And not a very good place."

Bolan handed her the mug and returned to get some coffee for himself.

"We buried alive?" Casper asked.

"Not as bad as it might have been," Bolan said. "We should be able to get through to Maple Lake."

"Count me out. No way I can make a trek in my condition," Casper said. "I'm not about to hold you back."

"That's crazy," Dukas said. "We should go together. We have to with those men out there looking for us."

"I'm a liability," Casper said.

"I'm not leaving you behind," Bolan said.

"*Go*. Get the hell out of here," Casper said. "Leave it too long, those trigger-happy idiots might still show up."

"And find you?" Bolan shook his head.

"Think straight, Cooper. All I'm doing is holding you back. Take me along, you're crippled. Can't do what you need to. They'll pick us off easy. On your own you can handle them."

Bolan knew Casper was right. He had no doubt the strike team would show up at first light.

His mind worked on a plan.

"This is how I'm going to do it, and I'm not running out on either of you," he said.

He outlined his idea, making it clear there was no other way.

Casper opened his mouth to protest, but Bolan had already turned aside, picking up the MP-5 and spare magazines. He took the M-16 and handed it to Casper, along with its extra mags. He passed the Glock to Dukas.

"Keep the shutters secure, door bolted. Make sure the smoke can be seen from the stack. That door is their only way in and if they get by me you have a clear line of sight."

"You sure about this?" Dukas asked.

"I don't see any other way. Just do what I said. Lie low and keep quiet."

Bolan had filled a mug with more coffee and drank as he talked and prepared. He zipped up his thick coat and pulled on his woolen cap and gloves. "Should be light in about a half hour," he said.

He opened the door just wide enough to slip through, Dukas following to secure it once he'd gone. She put a hand on his arm.

"Take it easy," she said.

The moment Bolan was gone she closed and bolted the door. Turning, she went to the stove and pushed in more wood, then sat beside it, her back to the wall. She dragged a blanket over her shoulders and held the Glock in her lap.

STAYING IN THE SHADOWS, Bolan crept close to the cabin, then eased into the brush and out of sight. He worked his way around until he was twenty feet from the cabin and able to blend into the dark shadows. He held the MP-5 close, eyes searching the shadows, and waited for the day—and the enemy—to come to him.

Bolan checked his firing position, feeling the movement of the wind and the drift of the falling snow. He knew which direction would bring them to his killing ground. That was what it would become, he'd resigned himself to the fact.

The sky had started to pale in the east. Snow continued to fall. The wind, ice chilled, stirred the brush, caught tree foliage and made it tremble. Bolan's eyes adjusted to the coming light. He scanned his field of fire, moving his eyes and nothing else. He kept his head down, exhaling gently so the vapor from his breath didn't show.

12

Jatko completed the call and broke contact. He did not look happy.

"I know that expression," Billingham said.

"They just found Zelliger's body. His weapons are gone and so is his transceiver. Bullets that killed him smashed his GPS unit."

"So nothing positive to report?"

"Zelliger exchanged fire before he died. Bullet marks showed on a tree trunk. And there was blood as well."

"So we assume one of them was wounded. Might slow them. Are the others following?" Billingham asked.

Jatko nodded. "They are now. Last night's whiteout stopped them cold. Only good thing is it would have stopped *them* as well," Jatko replied.

"Our people had the Humvees for protection. What did those three have? Unless they found cover maybe they froze to death."

Billingham peered at the on-screen map. Leaning over, Jatko indicated a spot.

"They were still moving in the general direction of Maple Lake yesterday."

"Maybe it's time we showed our faces there."

THERE WAS NO SUN. TO BOLAN'S right, snow fell from a sagging branch and made a soft sound on impact. Overhead, the wind gusted through the tops of the trees and created a ripple of noise. From the corner of his eye he could see the spiral of wood smoke coming from the cabin's chimney.

The Executioner had picked up movement in the trees on the far approach to the cabin—one armed figure, moving slowly. Then a second and third, spaced out as they emerged from the white forest. The lead man raised a hand and signaled for a stop.

Three so far. They all wore the same dark, combat-style clothing, weighed down with weapons and ancillary equipment. The lead man crouched, his two partners following suit, and spoke into his transceiver, waiting for a response. Two more figures materialized from the shadows, crouching like the others to reduce body bulk, waiting for the next command.

The lead man finished his conversation and clipped the transceiver to his belt again, then signaled his team to move forward.

No doubt they had seen the cabin and the scattered fragments of smoke.

Two of the incursion team angled in the direction of the cabin, weapons at the ready, while behind them the lead man swung his free arm to send the second pair in from the opposite direction.

Bolan raised the MP-5 and acquired his first target, stroking the trigger as soon as he had his man. Before the first man hit the ground Bolan had switched to his partner. The man responded swiftly, turning hard and bringing up his weapon, searching, the delay costing him his life. Bolan hit him with a burst to the chest that backflipped him into the snow. Angling the MP-5 around, Bolan let go with a sustained burst, the 9 mm slugs taking the second pair out, bringing them to their knees before they were able to seek and find the hidden shooter. As they slid to the bloody snow Bolan eased to one side, using trees as cover as he moved swiftly around the lead gunner. The man was twisting back and forth, seeking his elusive target, his transceiver in one hand as he yelled into the speaker. Bolan revealed himself, stepping out of deep cover, his MP-5 bearing down on the solitary figure, who for reasons of his own refused to quit and dropped the transceiver, raising his M-16 and cutting loose with a sustained burst that sprayed the area with 5.56 mm slugs.

Bolan hit him with a savage volley that cut the man down like straw in the wind, dumping his tattered and bleeding body on the ground.

The last echo of autofire drifted off into the trees. Wind rattled the brittle foliage, dislodging hard crusts of snow from the branches. Bolan's boots crunched over the ground layer as he moved from man to man, checking for signs of life and moving weapons clear. He had counted his targets and all were down.

Bolan moved quickly, aware that the last man to go down had called in. There was no way of knowing how many more were backing up this first team, and Bolan had no intention of staying to find out. He gathered extra ammo for the M-16, then headed back to the cabin. He announced himself and pushed his way inside the moment Dukas unbarred the door.

"We need to move," Bolan said. "One of them called in, so reinforcements might be on the way."

"More?" she asked. "Have they got an army out there?"

"Hiring people to do your dirty work comes cheap. Throw money at them, and they don't ask questions," Bolan replied.

Casper made an effort to stand, insisting he was capable of walking.

"Ten minutes out there and you'll have that leg bleeding again," Dukas said.

"So what? I get carried again?"

Bolan nodded. "Let's go, flyboy." He hoisted Casper over his shoulder. "If you have to hang on, just keep your hands from around my neck."

"If he complains," Dukas said, "I wouldn't mind being carried."

"Be more fun," Bolan said.

"Now you've hurt my feelings," Casper said.

They moved out quickly, aware that their pursuers could be close. Bolan found himself wishing the snowfall was heavier so it might bury their tracks, but that was something he couldn't control. They angled away from the cabin and headed cross-country, staying as close to cover as they could. Their progress was slow. The frozen top layer of snow wasn't strong enough to support their weight, and they were hampered by breaking through the crust, sinking into the deeper, softer snow beneath. Casper, though he stayed silent, was clearly in pain from each step. The partially closed wounds had opened, and even Bolan felt the warm blood that soaked through both Casper's and his clothing. He pushed his feelings to the back of his mind, ignoring the involuntary gasps of breath coming from the hurt pilot, and would have given heartfelt thanks to see Jack Grimaldi swooping down from the lead gray sky.

Dukas suggested they rest a couple of times, but she got a negative response from Bolan. He wanted to gain some distance before they took any kind of break. When he checked his watch for the first time, he saw they had been moving for almost an hour. He also noticed that the sky had darkened considerably and they were walking into more snow. It was increasing quickly, the drift pushing in at them, so that it would drop over the tracks they were leaving behind. It was a small comfort but at least a positive edge.

They came to a jagged ridge that ran across their path, east to west. Bolan saw Dukas studying the lay of the land, her eyes moving back and forth as she positioned herself against the distant and higher peaks.

"I was right," she said. There was no excitement in her voice, just the direct statement of fact. "Over that ridge we should be able to see the town. Only a few more miles."

Bolan simply nodded. It felt like too much effort to speak.

"Hang on, Bud, we're almost home," Bolan managed to say.

Casper grunted something unintelligible. He didn't even protest when Bolan hoisted him into a more comfortable position across his shoulders.

They moved off and started the long trek to the floor of the wide valley that encompassed Maple Lake. There were blurred outlines of buildings clustered along the south shore of the lake that gave the town its name. Moving forward, they skirted the edge of a long drop-off that led into a deep cut. Thick brush covered the slope, the shapes softened by the thick carpet of snow.

They had only been moving a few minutes when Bolan picked up the muffled sound of helicopter rotors. He stopped in his tracks, scanning the sky and saw that Dukas was doing the same.

"Which way is it coming in?" she asked.

Before Bolan could answer, the dark shape loomed out of the swirling snow, causing its own disturbance as it dropped down to intercept their path. Almost blinded by the powerful lash of the rotor wash and the icy rush of air chilling them, they backed away until the rim of the drop-off forced them to a halt.

Bolan eased Casper to the ground, hauling his MP-5 into position as the chopper, a dark-colored Sikorsky S-76, eased on. The side hatch slid open and revealed a number of armed figures hunched in the opening. Dark muzzles swung to line up on the three figures.

"No way," Bolan said, and before any of the men in

the chopper could react he opened fire, raking the hatch and the clustered figures with 9 mm defiance.

The burst of slugs hammered the chopper's sides. Some cut through clothing and into soft flesh. Two gunners fell out of view. A third fell forward, screaming in panic as he pitched through the hatch and crashed to the ground below.

Bolan saw Bud Casper rising to his feet, the M-16 in his hands. The man let go a wild yell and opened up with the automatic rifle, going for the canopy, the 5.56 mm slugs peppering the Plexiglas. The wounds on his leg and shoulder had burst open again, and bright blood glistened on his clothing, yet somewhere he had found the strength to deal himself into the fight. He raked the canopy again and it splintered.

The chopper pulled back, more gunmen showing in the hatch, weapons crackling as they tried to lock on to their targets. Bullets hit the ground around Bolan and Casper.

"Get her out of here," Casper yelled above the roar of the chopper.

As he spoke, he turned and lunged at Dukas, giving her no chance to resist. He slammed into her and pushed over the edge of the drop-off. She gave a scream of alarm as she tumbled down the long slope.

In the split second they faced each other, Bolan saw Casper was smiling. The pilot launched himself at Bolan and his attack was hard and uncompromising. The loose snow underfoot denied Bolan any purchase, and he felt himself stepping into air. The last thing he saw was Bud Casper's figure as the pilot turned back to face the returning chopper, his M-16 still crackling.

Other guns joined in, the sharp reports echoing in Bolan's consciousness as he hit the slope and bounced and rolled, out of control. He smashed through brush and thumped against hidden rocks. He felt the chill of thick snow on his face.

The fall seemed to last an eternity. He was helpless to fight against his descent. If he hadn't been wearing the MP-5 on a sling around his neck, he'd have lost the weapon. Sound thundered in his ears. A heavy rumbling. He realized it was disturbed snow following him down. If he survived the fall, he might still end up buried beneath tons of snow.

He tried to halt his descent, but there was nothing to hold on to. And then, suddenly, there was no ground beneath him. He was in the air, the sky spinning before his eyes. He was free-falling, then came to a sudden and shocking stop. Breath was forced from his lungs. Above him was the sky and falling snow. And still that ominous rumbling. Bolan turned toward the sound and saw a dense mass of snow racing toward him. He tried to move, to drag himself clear. He barely had time to turn onto his side before the avalanche hit and he was buried.

13

Lec Pavlic had reached Maple Lake in late afternoon, just ahead of the heavy storm. The wind was driving the snow down the slopes in solid sheets. It was impossible for him go any farther, and he'd considered parking and waiting out the storm. As Pavlic reached the final marker that told him the town lay three miles ahead, he spotted the Maple Lake Motel Lodge and eased the four-by-four off the road. He sat and watched the swirling snow blanketing the road and hiding everything in its path, recalling what the attendant at the gas station had told him. Three miles in the sort of weather closing in might easily turn into a nightmare. Pavlic decided to wait out the storm and try to get into town the next morning.

He climbed out of the four-by-four, locked it, and with his bag in his hand he tramped across to the office where he had seen a light. Pushing through the door he felt warmth close around him.

"Well, hellfire, you're the last thing I expected to see today." The speaker stood behind the desk. Short and stocky, with a mane of white hair framing a creased, tanned face, the man was clad in a check shirt and he grinned at Pavlic. "You drove all the way to Maple Lake just so you could stop here? I am flattered."

Pavlic dropped his bag at his feet and brushed snow from his coat.

"Well, I did drive all the way here. That part is true enough. I was hoping to reach the town tonight, but the way that snow is building up I do not think I could make it."

"Might only be three miles, but when that whiteout drops you won't get out of the parking lot. So it looks like we'll have your company tonight," the man said.

"That will be fine."

They spent a couple of minutes completing the formalities.

"Just the one night?" the clerk asked.

"Yes, I am hoping to complete my business quickly and return to Denver as soon as I can."

"That might not work out so easy. Looks like we're in for some heavy snow. Could be the road out gets blocked. If it does, you might be here for a while."

Pavlic had been aware of that possibility all the way in. He had tried not to allow it to deter him. Bad weather, or not, he had to get to Maple Lake and retrieve his package. He had to get his hands on the disk before Radin, Billingham or Granger. He knew that Billingham would have alerted Granger to Pavlic's presence in America. Once Granger had the story, Pavlic was sure he would move heaven and earth to find him.

Granger had the clout to employ shady characters

to do his dirty work. In his coveted position, well inside the high security shield that his work for the military and the government allowed, the man seemed impervious, able to command all kinds of covert help. He was so deeply entrenched that any misdemeanor could be dealt with, leaving him to his top secret, ultrasensitive work for the U.S.

Pavlic was a loner. Out in the cold, in more ways than one, and he was looking out for himself. The package that his niece had sent to Maple Lake meant too much for him to abandon. If he could regain possession and remove himself from the hands of his former friends, he stood at least a chance of getting out alive. If they reached it before he did, his life was over. Once destroyed all evidence would cease to exist and they would have won.

In his room he stood at the window watching the snowstorm close in. The world beyond the sealed glass had turned to blinding, obliterating white. Despite his mounting anxiety, Pavlic knew he would have to be patient. The only consolation was that it would be the same for anyone who might be searching for him. The weather was something not even the money and power of his enemies could control.

Stony Man Farm, Virginia

"OKAY," AARON KURTZMAN SAID. HE waved a folder in the air. "This is everything we've been able to gather on the information provided and it lays the groundwork for some interesting theories."

He waited until everyone in the room was paying attention.

"The floor's yours," Barbara Price said.

"Thorne Billingham, Milos Radin, Maric Jatko, Lec Pavlic. The tie-in for all of them seems to start around 1995, near the end of the Bosnian conflict and the reconstruction era. They were all involved in various facets of the administration. Advisers, financial, construction, contracting. That was a time when the area was in total confusion. So many agencies involved. Endless conferences. Planning committees. Funding, supplying, logistics. It was a mess.

"Move on a couple of years and all our above names have suddenly started to rise up the ladder in a loose conglomerate that has its fingers in a lot of pies. The main men are Radin, in Sarajevo and Thorne Billingham in the U.S. Now there's a third name to add. Ramsey Granger."

"One of the biggest military contractors? *That* Granger?" Carmen Delahunt asked.

Kurtzman nodded. "The same. His name came up during one of our sweeps. It appears he was one of the group back in 1995. We almost missed him first time around, but there was a tenuous connection with Lec Pavlic and when we dug deeper it seems he and Granger have met a lot over the years. Stepping back, we discovered that Granger was working with Billingham at the time."

"Nowadays our group is at the top of the heap. All are wealthy, well connected, and through a network of companies they're all in bed together. Granger is the most successful. He's a platinum member of the government contractors' club, a military supplier who's into every facet of research you can name. A lot of it very hush-hush. That means he has powerful backing. Granger has access to places and people most of us could only dream about."

"But what did these people do in 1995?" Akira Tokaido asked. "It had to have been pretty heavy to make them chase like this. Whatever Pavlic has in that package has caused some serious panic."

"I was thinking about that," Kurtzman said. "So I expanded my data searches for around that time in Bosnia. Not even certain what I was looking for until I hit on this."

He activated one of the wall monitors and they all watched as the information scrolled across the screen.

It gave details of six people who had vanished in that time slot. Five men and one woman. They had been listed as the victims of an unnamed ethnic execution squad. Their names were given, along with photographs.

"What makes you think these people might be involved with the Pavlic affair?" Price asked.

"I managed to access some data stored by a security agency in Sarajevo going back to the time the six vanished. The name of the woman who disappeared kept coming up, and I finally traced her to a section investigating rumors of money disappearing from various reconstruction funds. Seems she was doing undercover work looking into this allegation. The investigation wasn't getting much in the way of results, so it was side-lined. Then the building where the woman worked was hit by a stray artillery shell and demolished. A number of personnel were killed. When the department was eventually re-created, with new people, the fraud investigation was never resurrected. But some data had been filed on a central computer elsewhere and it's still there. Hasn't been accessed for years."

"Any names?"

"None of our main characters initially, but guys named Karel Medusku, Sev Malik and Jev Ritka. But he's out of the picture. Had an accident recently that left him in a coma. They all have associations with Milos Radin, going back to before the disappearance of the six. Now on their own these are just bits and pieces. Move them around and they start to connect. Maybe they're thin links, but there are too many of them to be coincidence."

"We going to follow this through?" Tokaido asked.

"What do you think?"

"Silly question, boss. I'll get right on it."

"I'm going to try and make some contact with the authorities in Sarajevo," Kurtzman said. "See if they have any back story on all this."

14

The Executioner could feel someone tugging at his arm. He wanted to stay where he was. It felt good. Soft and warm. But the distant voice was getting louder, and he felt sure he knew it. He opened his eyes.

Erika Dukas was bending over him, shaking his shoulder, and she was yelling at him to wake up and get his butt moving.

Bolan got to his feet, shaking off the surplus snow.

"Might be wise to stop yelling," he said. "Sound carries up here."

"Thanks for your help, how are you, might be a better start," she snapped.

"You're right," he said. "Hey, Erika, how are you? And thanks for digging me out."

She grinned suddenly, turning to scan the slope they had fallen down. Bolan didn't follow her gaze. He was looking at the raw scrape on the side of her head, just below the hairline. Blood had streamed down her face, running into her collar. He caught her shoulders and drew her closer.

"Why, Matt, this is so sudden and me looking a real mess," she said, laughing.

He gently inspected the gash. She became aware of the pain, moving her head a little. "I'm not going to hurt you," he said.

"I know that."

He quickly opened her backpack and pulled out a strip of material he could use to clean the wound. From more of the material he made a small pad, got her to hold it over the gash while he wound a strip around her head to hold it in position.

"The Colorado fashion accessory no girl should be without," she quipped.

Bolan nodded. He became businesslike immediately, taking the MP-5 and checking it thoroughly. He made sure the action was clear and undamaged, the barrel free of hard-packed snow. He repeated the procedure with the M-16 Dukas had over her shoulder.

"How did you find me?" he asked.

"I landed in some thick brush over there. The avalanche missed me completely. I was watching and saw where you landed."

"Any other injuries?" he asked.

"By tomorrow I'm going to have bruises in places I never had them before." She paused. "We were lucky. What about Bud? Is he dead?"

"I have no idea. Right now, harsh as it might sound, we have to forget about him and think of ourselves. What he did saved our lives, so we have to make sure it wasn't wasted. You understand, Erika?"

She nodded. "I'm getting used to putting my grieving on the back burner. When this is over, you're going to have to provide me with a giant box of tissue."

"Let's move out," Bolan said.

As they made their way, Dukas asked, "You recognize anyone in that helicopter?"

"No, but I did see the logo just under the pilot's canopy before the shooting started. That chopper belonged to Granger Industries."

"Isn't he a big name in military contracting? Design and development in weapons and such?" Dukas asked.

"More than big. Ramsey Granger is the hottest player in the game at the moment. Very ambitious. Few scruples. Lots of friends in high places."

"They'll be coming for us, won't they?" she asked.

"You could be a big threat until they know whether or not you learned anything," Bolan said.

The soft hiss of sliding snow warned them company was on its way. Bolan saw it was coming from the steep slope behind them. Their pursuers were attempting the fast way down, but there was no way they could do it in total silence. He turned to Erika, indicating a dip in the ground.

"In there and stay out of sight."

She obeyed immediately, circling the depression until she was on its far side, then dropped into the hollow.

Bolan cocked the MP-5, moving along the base of the slope until he was level with the moving traces of snow. Following it up the slope he saw three armed men rappelling down. They saw him, and one let loose with a burst from the submachine gun he was holding in his left hand. The slugs pounded the snow yards off target.

Bolan raised his weapon and returned fire. There was no hesitation in his actions. The lines had been drawn and the battle engaged. That was the way they wanted it, so Bolan would let them see what real war meant.

He triggered in the direction of the shooter and saw his 9 mm slugs punch into the man's upper body. The shooter jerked, his rappelling line locked, so he stayed where he was, blood spattering the snow below him. The moment he'd fired Bolan tracked in on the other two, the MP-5 crackling repeatedly. He saw the suspended figures jerk and writhe, trapped on the exposed slope. The bullets blew dark flecks from their clothing and bright blood from their flesh as the Executioner's killing fire struck home. One had failed to lock his line and he plunged down the slope. He landed hard, his body sprawled in death.

"Go," Bolan said to Dukas.

She scrambled to her feet, and they ran as fast as they could through the crust of frozen snow, knowing there would be other gunners behind them.

Bolan directed them to a stand of trees, pale and ghostly where the snow had frozen to trunks and limbs. As they broke into the shadowed stand, autofire opened up behind them. Bolan stood his ground, bracing himself against a sturdy trunk and returning fire. He caught the lead shooter, chest high, the impact kicking the man off his feet, then changed aim and put another man down with shots that cored through hip and thigh.

Dukas started to fire her M-16. When Bolan glanced around, he saw a pair of shooters angling in from his blind side. He saw one go down, taking a couple of 5.56 mm slugs. The other shooter turned aside, moving back out of range.

Bolan raked his line with more 9 mm fire, halting their progress.

"Move on," he said.

Dukas backed deeper into the timber, still firing until Bolan told her to save her ammunition.

Snapping in a fresh magazine he followed in her footsteps, watching her back as they moved. If Billingham and company wanted to get their hands on Erika Dukas, they were going to have to pay one hell of a price for that privilege.

The cat and mouse game stayed constant as Bolan and Dukas pushed their way deeper into the timber that covered the area. The falling snow was becoming heavier. The dense forest growth slowed its descent to the ground, but it was still getting through.

Closer to Maple Lake the terrain evened out a little. The thick snow underfoot kept movement measured and tedious. If they tried to rush, the snow held them back, so they were careful. Bolan noticed the temperature had risen slightly. It was cold, but it had become bearable.

After almost an hour he called a halt and they crouched in the shadow of an overhang.

"Think we've lost them?" Dukas asked, looking around.

"They're still out there. They have their orders, and

they'll stick to them. Weather isn't making it any easier for them. As long as this snow keeps falling, they'll have a hard time picking up our tracks. It's all we can depend on." He put a firm hand on her shoulder. "You holding up?"

"One way or another."

Bolan caught a sound. He checked out the way ahead.

"Sounds like an engine," Dukas said.

"Ahead of us." He peered into the falling snow. "Coming from that way. Humvee."

He indicated a long draw that made a shallow furrow in the landscape.

"Maybe they'll offer us a ride," Dukas said wearily.

"Yeah. But not the way you might expect. Use those trees for cover until the Humvee comes out of the draw. Show yourself long enough so they see you. The minute they move to step out you get back under cover. Understand?"

Dukas followed his instructions and headed for the timberline. Glancing back she saw that her companion had vanished, but she knew well enough that he was not far away. She eased between the thick trunks and waited, hearing the deep rumble draw closer.

Bolan saw the Humvee as it barreled out of the draw, wheels kicking up great showers of dirty snow. The driver had laid on the power to mount the final rise where the draw merged with the flatter terrain and the huge vehicle burst into view. It slammed on the ground, the rear sliding for a moment until the driver brought it back under control.

The man next to the driver threw out a warning hand as he spotted Dukas moving. She ducked quickly back into the tree cover as the Humvee slithered to a halt. The passenger door flew open and an armed man jumped out, leveling his M-16. The driver was seconds behind, reaching back to grab his own weapon.

The moment the men were out of the vehicle, Bolan made his move, leaning out from his cover and triggering a burst into the passenger that dropped him where he stood, then angling the muzzle across the Humvee's hood to track the driver. The man recovered quickly, turning his M-16 in Bolan's direction and even squeezing off a short bust before the Executioner's weapon snapped again. The 9 mm slugs took him high in the chest and throat, spinning him away from the Humvee in a bloody spray and dropping him facedown in the snow.

Bolan waved for Dukas to stay where she was while he checked out the vehicle for other gunners. He slid down the steep bank and crossed to the Humvee. After checking the vehicle, he collected the dead men's weapons and extra ammunition. He deposited the equipment inside the Humvee, then waved Dukas in. She joined him and climbed directly inside, slamming the door. Bolan got in behind the wheel.

"Hurry up and close that door," she said. "I'll never be warm again."

Bolan drove off, working the heavy all-terrain vehicle around until he had it pointed in the direction of Maple Lake.

"I don't believe this," Dukas murmured. "We might actually make it before the sun goes down."

"Arriving is the important part," Bolan said, "not how long it takes."

"Head for the south edge of town," Dukas said. "The general store and post office is at the far side. The sheriff's office midway along. Do you think we're going to be there before Billingham's group?"

"If they've figured out where Tira sent the package, they might already be making a play for it," Bolan said.

"I'd hate to lose out now after everything we've been through. I wanted to get hold of that package for Tira's sake. We miss that chance, she died for nothing."

"It isn't over yet," the Executioner said.

BOLAN RAN THE HUMVEE OFF the track and parked beneath a dense and heavy mass of thick brush. He drove deep into the center of the thicket, the mass of foliage closing in around the vehicle, hiding it from view. The disturbed snow from the foliage cascaded down over the ATV as he cut the engine and they sat in the silence that descended over them. Falling snow began to cover the tire marks.

"What? Back on foot? I just got comfortable again," Dukas said.

"Only for me," Bolan replied.

"I'm not going to like this am I?"

"I need to do this fast. Don't take it the wrong way, Erika, but distractions will slow me down. And what I have to do might not sit easy for you."

"Fine, go and do whatever you have to do. Just don't leave me out here too long or I might decide to come charging in to rescue you."

He saw the smile on her lips, but there was no way she could hide the concern in her eyes.

Bolan quietly checked his weapons. He showed Dukas the compact transceiver he had set to a new frequency.

"Keep it close. If I call you'll know it's safe to come in. Otherwise keep out of sight. Stay inside the vehicle, but keep alert. If you figure they might get close enough to spot you, get out and bury yourself somewhere until any threats move on. I won't pretend this isn't a risky time, but we've come through this far. Do you trust me?"

"Over the past couple of days haven't you shown me a good time?" she said.

Making light of the situation was her way of covering how she felt. Bolan understood that and he admired her for it.

"You are one hell of a lady, Dukas."

He moved to leave and she reached out to stop him, leaning over to kiss him. "Damn you, Cooper, don't you forget to come back in one piece."

"You can count on that," he said brusquely, and he was gone, a brief flurry of falling snow drifting into the Humvee as he left the vehicle.

The heavy brush settled back in place as he drifted out of her sight, and she was alone, entombed in the white cocoon of snow and foliage and surrounded by utter silence. She was confident he would be fine. He would succeed and come back for her. Really alone for the first time she felt the breathless rush of events crowd her in a instant. She felt tears rise, overcome by the emotions she had been bottling up. She allowed it to happen, not out of pity for herself but because someone had to weep for those who had already paid the price of other men's brutality.

THE EXECUTIONER ALMOST WALKED into the first of the perimeter guards. The other man was just as surprised, and it came down to who recovered faster.

The falling snow and the cathedral silence that blanketed the area had reduced footfalls to nothing. Bolan, acknowledging to a dragging weariness, had sensed the guard's presence a scant second before he saw the guy.

They moved together, each hoping to gain the advantage in that precious sliver of time.

The guard chose to unlimber his M-16, wasting his opportunity, and Bolan's own move countered it in an instant. His own weapon was in his left hand, leaving the right free. Bolan made a solid fist and drove it into the guard's face, slamming the man backward, his nose flattened and gushing blood. He swung again, this time a back fist that crunched against the jaw, smashing it from its setting and loosening a number of teeth. He followed through with another blow that snapped the man's head back and drove him against the trunk of a tree. The dazed guard barely registered the impact when Bolan drove the heel of his hand below his jaw and rocked his head back into the solid trunk. As the guard went down, Bolan bent over him, removed all his weapons and threw them into the surrounding foliage.

So what were you watching over, buddy? he wondered.

Bolan edged forward cautiously. One guard could mean more. He was back on full alert, the adrenaline surge snapping him out of his lethargy. His diligence was rewarded when he saw the trees thinning out to reveal a large natural clearing—and the dark bulk of a helicopter. Bolan recognized the configuration. He also spotted the bullet holes in the fuselage and canopy, and the Granger Industries logo.

As he walked into the clearing, someone shouted a warning.

The rattle of autofire shattered the forest calm. Then shouted orders. Then anger. Not a little panic. Bolan stalked the clearing, his MP-5 dealing out cleansing fire. He ignored any considerations of personal safety. He knew these men, paid by those higher up, were willing to deal out suffering and death so that the *important* men could sleep soundly in their beds. He was there to ensure the sleep they desired would be filled with nightmares. Bolan didn't bring absolution. He delivered retribution.

Granger, Billingham and Radin had rolled the dice—now they were about to reap the rewards.

15

"Your luck's changing, Mr. Pavlic."

Pavlic followed the man's gaze. Beyond the window the snowed in landscape seemed less threatening than it had the previous day. The snow was still swirling across the lodge's parking lot, but it was nowhere near as heavy as before.

"Yes, it does appear so. I think I should complete my business and return to Denver."

"You finish your coffee and I'll get your bill ready."

"Thank you. Oh, when does the post office open? I should have a package waiting there for me. My company sent it on ahead for me a few days ago."

"General store opens at nine this time of year, so it'll be up for business by the time you make it into town."

Pavlic nodded. He topped up his coffee and considered what he would do once he had the disk back in his possession. The important thing was to lose himself somewhere within the vast American continent while he made definite plans for the future.

A return to his own country was out of the question. His former colleagues were out to eliminate him. He was going to have to make himself an exile, but with the money he had salted away at least he'd be comfortable.

Pavlic regretted he had no weapon to protect himself. His rapid departure from Sarajevo had not allowed him the opportunity to arrange anything. His commercial flights had meant there had been no way to carry a gun even if he'd had one. This was his first visit to Colorado, so there were no contacts he could turn to. When he considered the matter, he realized that unlike the others he had never needed to arm himself. The circles they ran in carried risks, and special work done for them over the years called for contacts who could acquire weapons if and when required. Compared to them, he was an innocent abroad.

Pavlic had not forgotten the long reach of his ex-partners. For all he knew they could have discovered his destination and might already be on their way to interrupt him. They might already be waiting for him in Maple Lake.

He drove out of the parking lot and took the road to Maple Lake. The snow was pristinely white and smooth, the ever-present wind skating frozen particles across it like sand in a desert.

He drove slowly, aware that the surface beneath his wheels had been hard frozen during the night. He reached the flat, straight run that led in toward the main street and had yet to see any other vehicles, or people. He drove by a few timber houses, then a gas station. There was a gap and then he saw the building that bore the sign Maple Lake General Store.

Pavlic eased off the gas pedal and gently touched the brake pedal, easing the SUV to a stop alongside the store. He could see movement inside. He climbed out of the vehicle, feeling the chill bite of the wind and the sting of frozen snow particles against his cheek.

THE TOTAL WAS FIVE DEAD and one wounded.

Bolan found plastic cuffs among the blood-spattered equipment inside the chopper. He secured the wounded mercenary to a fixed support and let the man think about his position for a while.

In the meantime Bolan checked out the Sikorsky's communication setup and it was as up-to-date as anything he'd seen. With one eye on the prisoner Bolan worked the radio, adjusting the digital settings to the Stony Man frequency. He put out a call and waited while the satellite feed and various cutouts connected him with the Farm.

"Striker, what the hell has been going on?" Hal Brognola asked.

"You got the background?"

"Damn it, yes, but we've been worried about the pair of you. How's Erika?"

"We're fine."

"That storm still got you bottled in?"

"Not just the storm. We have some hostiles roaming the woods. Courtesy of Ramsey Granger."

"You found this package yet?"

"No. There've been some distractions along the way

and the game isn't over yet. I don't anticipate getting reinforcements anytime soon."

"Don't be too sure about that. Jack is on the way. I managed to fix an Air Force ride for him to a base in Colorado. Shouldn"t be too much of a jump from there to your mountain retreat."

"I'm not holding my breath. Weather's still undecided up here," Bolan said.

"Looks like a real can of worms was opened by this Lec Pavlic. He's caused one hell of a panic. Now we have the Sarajevo cops begging for information. Once Kurtzman started digging bells and whistles started going off over there. When this breaks, you'll be able to monitor the reaction on the Richter scale. Brognola filled Bolan in on Kurtzman's findings."

"Hal, don't write these people off that easy. Especially Granger. The man has connections in very high places. The pull he has within the Defense Department will give him heavy protection," Bolan said.

"If what we suspect is true, it's not going to be easy sailing for these people."

"Word of mouth isn't going to swing it, Hal. We have to have solid evidence. Without it Granger's lawyers walk him free. We both know that."

The man from Justice sighed.

"I'm going for that package, Hal. If what we believe is true then we owe it to those people who died. And to Erika's friend, Tira. She had nothing to do with any of this but they killed her like she was nothing. And they threatened Erika's life too."

"Stay safe, Striker. We want you both back alive and well," Brognola said.

"Tell Jack to check south of Maple Lake for Bud Casper. He saved us. Gave us the chance to make a break. He went down fighting."

Bolan broke the connection.

He went back to where his prisoner sat glowering. The man's wounded left arm was still bleeding, so Bolan located a first-aid kit and tended to it. The man protested but one look at Bolan's grim face shut him up.

"So where's the big man himself?" Bolan asked.

"Don't know what you mean."

"Granger must be paying you well. Or is there a nondisclosure clause in your contract?"

"You always talk in fucking riddles?" the man said.

"The chopper belongs to Granger Industries. It's written on the side. Or do I guess you just picked it up at a Hertz rental?"

"You realize who you're bucking here?"

"Some poorly trained, overpaid help Granger picked up on the cheap."

"The hell with you. All you got is lucky," the prisoner said.

The man fell silent, defiantly staring over Bolan's shoulder.

Bolan checked his weapons. There was an ample supply of extra ordnance inside the chopper. He bulked up on ammunition for his MP-5. The M-16 A-3s that seemed to be the favored weapon of the opposition were available, secured in racks. Bolan found a couple fitted with M-203 grenade launchers. He chose one and slung a bandolier holding loads for the weapon around his neck, adding magazines for the rifle itself. With his weapons locked and loaded Bolan turned to leave.

"You going to fight a war, or something?" the prisoner asked with a sneer.

"Or something," the Executioner said, then stepped out of the helicopter and was swallowed by the falling snow.

THE SHERIFF OF MAPLE LAKE WAS embarrassed and angry. He had walked into his own department, along with one of his deputies and the town doctor, to find themselves under the guns of hooded strangers who had taken over the building.

Sheriff Garrett's brusque demand to be told what was going on earned him a bruised jaw from one of the armed invaders.

"That," Jatko said, "is what is going on, Sheriff. Now sit the fuck down and stay quiet."

Moving to the far side of the large office Jatko took out his transceiver, contacting Billingham. "We have the local cops under our control. And the doctor," he said.

"There shouldn't be much resistance from anyone else. According to our information, there are only a few local residents left in the town. Leave the sheriff's department guarded and go find that store where the post office is located. Maric, get that damned package so we can leave this place," Billingham said.

"You heard from Granger?"

"Only that his people have made contact with our fugitives. One down, but the big man and that Dukas woman are still loose."

"Well, let him chase them around the damned mountains. Now we have the town shut down we can collect the package," Jatko said.

"Knowing Ramsey, he'll want to be around when the package surfaces too."

"If I didn't know you better, Thorne, I'd have to say there's a trace of mistrust in your voice."

Billingham's hesitation spoke volumes. A mistrustful individual himself, Jatko had an insight into Billingham's train of thought. "You feel he might want to snatch the package for himself? Is that it?"

"Why would he, Maric?" Billingham asked, planting the seed in Jatko's mind. "What would it gain him?"

Jatko laughed.

"You know what it would give him, Thorne. Total control over the whole group. Every one of us. He could dangle that information over our heads so we dance to his tune whenever he wants. Of course, we are only speculating. Granger is a friend. He would never turn against us."

"Maric, get to that package *now*," Billingham shouted.

MACK BOLAN WATCHED THE ARRIVAL of the town sheriff, his deputy and a civilian who carried what looked like a medical bag. He studied the stone-and-timber building with its wide front window that had a grille of fine metal mesh on the inside. There was a tall radio mast rising above the roofline. There were three SUVs parked out front, black and white, bearing the logo of the Maple Lake Sheriff's Department. When Bolan edged around the corner of the deserted building that was providing his cover, he spotted a civilian Humvee.

Making a wide loop he crossed the street and came in against the end wall of the building. Edging around the corner, Bolan crept to where he could peer in through the front window.

Maple Lake's law enforcement and the civilian were being held at gunpoint by five armed men. One of the deputies, a young woman, had bloodstains down the front of her tan shirt. A male deputy had a head wound. Bolan pulled back, crouching beside the wall. He was considering his options when he heard the front door open and he saw three of the men leave the building, weapons clearly visible. One of them was speaking into a transceiver. They cleared the building and walked along the street, making slow progress through the drifts and the prevailing wind. Bolan watched them go, waiting until they were lost in the swirling snowfall.

He moved across the parking area until he was at the far side, closer to the main door. Taking the M-16 Bolan loaded an HEDP M-433 grenade into the M-203 launcher. He took aim at the furthest of the patrol vehicles and hit the lower rear with the grenade. The M-433 round ripped into the vehicle with ease. The gas tank blew, throwing a ball of flame into the air. Bolan ducked low as debris was hurled across the parking lot, bouncing and clattering as it landed. Tendrils of flaming gasoline spewed in all directions.

The expected reaction occurred quickly. The office's front doors opened and one of the remaining pair of masked men stood framed in the opening, staring at the blazing wreck. He took a hesitant step forward, checking the immediate area, and reached for the transceiver clipped to his belt.

Bolan hit him with an autoburst from the M-16, the impact spinning the guy and bouncing him off the door frame as he went down. The Executioner stepped over the body and went inside, his eyes scanning for the other masked intruder. He saw the dark bulk as the man rushed forward, his rifle raised and belching rounds. The stream of 5.56 mm slugs chewed plaster from the wall above Bolan's head as he dropped to a crouch, angling his own weapon and cutting the shooting off at waist level. The raider gasped, twisting in agony as the slugs chewed into his torso. Bolan hit him a second time, jacking out another burst that dropped the man to the floor in a bloody heap, his rifle clattering across the smooth wood floor.

Bolan turned and took hold of the first raider, dragging him inside so he could close and secure the doors.

"Sheriff?"

"That's me," Garrett snapped. "Now you want to tell me what the hell is going on? And who you are?"

"Matt Cooper, Justice Department. No time to go into full details now, Sheriff. The main problem you have are the armed men running loose in your town and the surrounding area. I suggest you arm your people, because the men who left are going to be back fast."

Garrett turned to snap orders to his people. The man Bolan had guessed correctly as the local doctor went to check on the deputy Jatko's men had worked over.

"Sheriff, where is your general store? The one that has the post office?" Bolan asked.

"This side of the street, at the far end. Post office? You expecting mail?"

Bolan nodded.

"Special delivery. It's why these people are here. Something they want to get their hands on pretty badly. Enough to kill for."

Bolan eased the door open and slipped through before Garrett could ask him any more questions.

"THIS COULD HAVE A BAD domino effect, Lee," Granger said.

"How so?" Marker asked.

"If it comes out I was involved, the whole organization will be under a microscope. Every damn deal, every contract will be viewed as tainted. I have enemies. They'll use the revelations as an excuse to go for me. They'll also use it to go for the people I do business with. You know what Washington is like. A bunch of sharks just circling, waiting for a whiff of blood so they can go in for the kill. See a chance and make your play. If someone starts digging and uncovers the deals we make off the books, I may not be able to protect those people."

"The kickback brigade?" Marker smiled. "They were willing enough to take your money. What's the current tally? One naval commander and a couple of senior Army personnel. We still dealing with that congressman? The one who keeps reminding you he'll be available for a board post when his political career runs its course?"

"They all want something, Lee. Money. Power. The job handouts with the cars and all-expenses paid."

"So why worry about them? Every damn one has a deal to hide."

"The minute the warning signs flash they'll run for the hills, do everything to cover their backs, hide the offshore accounts. It'll be total denial time. They'll disassociate themselves from anything to do with me, or Granger Industries."

"Time to find out who your real friends are."

Granger forced a smile. "I won't have any, Lee. I'm not naive enough to believe any of those bastards will stick by me. They'll drop me so fast the thud will be heard the length of the Shenandoah Valley."

"Know what I'd do if they screwed me like that? Send a file on every one of them to CNN. With pictures."

"Lee, I never realized you had such a vivid imagination."

"We all have to have a hobby."

"Lee, have another chopper ready. Billingham screwed up with the first one. It's time we made our presence felt in Maple Lake. Be there for the troops."

16

The Executioner cleared the building, turning to make his way around to the rear. Stone chips peppered the air just ahead of the sound of autofire and Bolan knew he'd been tagged. He kept moving and started along the back lots of Maple Lake.

The snow hampered his movements. He used whatever cover was available. Store sheds, empty cases. The metal waste containers behind each store.

Slugs hammered at the Dumpster he was passing near the far end of the street. Bolan felt one snap past his head when it bounced off the thick metal. He turned suddenly, facing the oncoming shooters and caught them off guard.

Bolan's finger stroked the trigger of the M-16, the assault rifle jacking out hard bursts of 5.56 mm slugs. He caught the lead shooter just above the waist, running the continuous volley up into the man's chest, then arced the muzzle around and repeated the move with the second guy. This one made an effort to turn, his body twisting in a violent attempt at escape. But there was no avoiding the Executioner's lethal fire.

The slugs cored into his side and tore his ribs to splinters before driving metal and bone into his lungs, pitching him facedown in the blood-frothed snow.

Bolan moved on, along the back lots, the general store looming large as he reached the place. There was a small loading bay and steps leading to a door. He went up the steps, raised a booted foot and kicked the door open. It smashed back against the inner wall and he went in, heading for the access that would take him into the store proper.

He emerged behind the counter, confronted by the alarmed store owner, who took one look at the tall, dark clad figure and the cluster of weapons he carried.

Bolan's eye had caught a figure leaving through the front door. The man looked over his shoulder at him, then stepped outside quickly.

"He come for a package sent from Washington?" Bolan asked.

"Yeah. How did you know?"

Bolan cut around the counter and made for the door, ejecting the M-16's magazine and snapping in a fresh one.

As he reached the door he saw Lec Pavlic on the top step of the store, pausing as someone called out in Serbian.

"Pavlic. There is nowhere else to run."

PAVLIC TURNED AS HE HEARD the voice of Maric Jatko.

The words had a chill finality to them. Pavlic sensed closure. An end to something that had started back in

1995 on a gray, rain-chilled day deep in the bleak forest beyond Sarajevo.

Jatko emerged from the swirling snow, flanked by a pair of shooters. Jatko himself carried a weapon. He would kill Pavlic and take the package. The evidence would be destroyed and nothing would change.

"The package, Pavlic. Give it to me."

"So you can kill me too?"

"I will anyway. As easily as that idiot Tivik. And the Malivik girl. Pretty young thing before we dealt with her. Your niece, I believe? Now give the fucking thing to me."

"No, Pavlic, give *me* the package."

This time the voice came from behind Pavlic, a deep, commanding American voice. Pavlic threw a glance over his shoulder and saw the Executioner emerge from the store.

"Who are you?" he asked.

"U.S. Justice Department. Give me the package, and I'll make sure it gets into the right hands."

The exchange lasted no more than a few seconds. Enough time though for Jatko to become aware of Bolan's presence. Time too for Pavlic to be plagued with doubt.

"Deal with him," Jatko snapped at Milic and Anton. "I'll go after Pavlic."

Bolan spotted the move even as it began. He brought the M-16 in line and the weapon was jacking out hard shots even as the shooters faced off. Bolan stitched the pair left to right, then back again, forcing them to their knees in bloody supplication. As he stepped across the top step, Bolan put a final burst into each man—head shots that confirmed their fate.

THE APPEARANCE OF THE BIG American caught Maric Jatko off guard. The man had once again defied everything that stood against him. He seemed to possess an uncanny knack of turning up at the most inappropriate moments.

Jatko's surprise evaporated as quickly as it formed. He had more important considerations to attend to—namely gaining possession of Pavlic's package.

The rattle of autofire created a brassy background sound as Jatko moved in Pavlic's direction. Pavlic had galvanized himself into movement the moment the shooting started. He was making his way to the four-by-four he had arrived in. Jatko could see the package clutched in his hands.

Jatko's anger burned as he raised his M-16 and fired. He saw Pavlic stumble as the slugs tore through his left shoulder, tearing out a chunk of flesh. He stumbled, almost going down. He regained his balance as Jatko fired again. The slugs pounded against the four-by-four's side, tearing jagged holes in the metal, spitting across the hood and cracking the windshield. Then Jatko steadied his aim and triggered an even longer burst that hit Pavlic between the shoulders, slamming him facedown in the bloody snow, his body writhing. Still firing, Jatko moved in the direction of the downed figure.

He sensed movement off to his right, turning to

see Bolan a fraction of a second before the Executioner's M-16 crackled, the line of 5.56 mm slugs burning into Jatko's chest. The impact took his breath, shock spreading rapidly, and Jatko was down, thrashing in agony. His own weapon had dropped from his hands and there was nothing he could do to regain it. He saw the tall American as Bolan stood over him. Jatko tasted blood in his mouth. He wanted to speak but there were no words.

"THERE," MILOS RADIN SAID, pointing through the windshield.

The driver of the Humvee nodded, putting his foot down as they rolled along the main street. As they passed the sheriff's office they saw the burned wreck of a vehicle and saw armed officers moving out from the building.

"What do we do?" the driver asked.

Billingham, in the rear of the vehicle, leaned forward.

"*Do?* We keep going. Jatko called and said he had Pavlic. That's what we're here for. No change there."

At the far end of the street they were witness to the brief exchange of fire between Bolan and Jatko's group. In a clear moment, as the wind dispersed the falling snow, Billingham recognized Lec Pavlic in the moment he was shot down, and then Jatko himself was hit. Radin powered down his window and leaned out, using his pistol in an attempt to take out the American, but firing from a moving vehicle did little to enhance his aim and his shots were wild.

Bolan heard the roar of the Humvee and saw it

speeding in his direction. He raised the M-16, slipping his finger behind the trigger of the M-203 launcher. His finger eased back and fired off the HEDP round. It arced across the distance, hitting the Humvee. The explosion lifted the vehicle and flipped it on its side, shattered debris flying from the stricken vehicle. Flames licked along the underside, igniting leaking fuel. Bolan saw a bloody shape emerge from one of the rear doors, climbing awkwardly out of the upturned vehicle. In the flickering glare of the burning fuel he made out the bloody features of Thorne Billingham. The man was clutching a pistol in one hand. Bolan closed in, raising the muzzle of the M-16, and laid a fast burst into the man's upper body. Billingham stiffened, then fell back inside the wrecked Humvee, where Milos Radin lay dead, a chunk of metal buried deep inside his skull.

Bolan turned and walked back to where Pavlic lay. There was no need for a close inspection. Jatko's fire had ripped into his back and as Pavlic went down the burst had taken away the back of his skull.

Reaching down, Bolan picked up the package, turning it over in his hand. It didn't look as if it could blow the lid off a long-term conspiracy of silence. But Bolan had learned long ago that appearances were often deceptive.

Bolan looked up when he heard the rising sound of rotors.

The dark shape of a helicopter was moving in to hover at the end of the street. He recognized the profile.

Another Sikorsky S-76. The chopper swung in and dropped to within a couple of feet, the wash fanning the flames from the burning Humvee, scattering smoke and snow into a frenzy.

Bolan raised his M-16 as he saw the side hatch slide open to reveal an armed man. A second gunner appeared. The Executioner knew the face. Ramsey Granger. A big man, hard faced. There was an expression of triumph, as if he had a prize worth showing.

Granger reached behind him and pulled someone from inside the compartment so Bolan could see.

Erika Dukas.

And then Granger raised his hand and pressed the muzzle of a pistol to her head.

17

Her crestfallen expression said it all. Dukas was slumped in the corner of the chopper's cargo section, hands resting on her raised knees. Her natural resilience was gone.

Bolan sat on the opposite side. At the sound of her voice he drew his gaze from the armed men casually watching him. One of them had his assault rifle trained on Bolan.

"Granger has better equipment than I figured," Bolan said. "He supplies the military, so he should be able to lay his hands on the best there is."

"I thought I was well hidden."

"Infrared. Ultrasonics. Heat source scanners. He indicated the electronic setup installed at the front of the aircraft. "It happens." He lowered his voice. "We're not through yet."

Granger made his way to where the prisoners sat and stood over Bolan. He wore dark pants, all-weather boots and an expensive leather jacket over a crewneck sweater. He looked every inch the successful business magnate. His rugged face, tanned and starting to show a dark stubble, was set. Cold eyes stared out on a world he saw as his personal domain.

"You've been busy," he said. "You've caused me a great deal of time and money, not to mention placing me in a difficult position."

Bolan remained silent.

"Tell me something. I don't believe Cooper is your real name. What should I call you?"

"Irresistible?"

Granger's cheeks showed a flush of anger at Bolan's mocking response. The gibe was strengthened by a smothered laugh from Dukas.

Granger leaned forward and delivered a hard punch that crunched against Bolan's left cheek. The blow was unrestrained, delivered with a savage intent and it snapped Bolan's head back. Granger struck again, this time with his right fist, across Bolan's jaw, tearing the flesh and drawing blood.

"You're a big man when your opponent can't fight back," Dukas said, making her contempt plain. "Or woman."

Granger turned to face her, breathing hard.

"Watch that mouth, Miss Dukas. Recall what happened to your late friend Tira Malivik."

"The level you and your friends stoop to, Granger, I wouldn't expect anything else."

"Then you should know what to *expect* once we touch down."

Bolan, recovering from Granger's attack, spit blood

from his mouth. "You have your package. What do you need with us?" he asked, challenging Granger.

"I need to know the information relating to Pavlic's disk hasn't gone further. If it has, I want to know where and to whom. It's damage control. If I have details, I can attempt to suppress that knowledge. You're a smart man. Figure it out. Containment. Information restriction. Call it what you like. I'm into self-preservation."

"And to hell with how many innocent people get hurt in the process?" Bolan asked.

"*Innocent?* We live in the twenty-first century. The last innocent went out decades ago. This society thrives on deceit and corruption, and you damn well know it."

"It only happens if we stand by and do nothing."

"Jesus, I think he believes that, too," Lee Marker said as he joined his employer.

"We have a true idealist among us, Lee," Granger said.

"Pilot says we should clear the storm front in a few minutes. Once we drop down to the foothills the weather should ease off. After that a steady flight to the facility," Marker whispered.

Bolan managed to pick up most of the conversation. He needed to get himself and Dukas off the helicopter before it reached the confines of Granger's facility.

He saw Granger and Marker move toward the front of the cabin section. He made a final assessment of the opposition.

Two up front—pilot and copilot. Granger and Marker. Five armed men in combat gear taking up the seats at the fore end of the passenger compartment, with one of them facing Bolan and Dukas.

He glanced at Dukas. For the first time since he been forced aboard he clearly saw the fresh bruises on her face. A bloody lip. She forced a crooked smile at him.

He turned to look out the side port, seeing the clear day emerging as the Sikorsky swooped down the mountain slopes. The terrain below was wide and empty, tracts of timber and wild undergrowth. To their right he caught the flicker of water between the trees.

Bolan's mind was working overtime. Whatever he did would be drastic, risky and with no guarantee of success. But the alternative was no better. Whatever the result of his intended interrogation, Granger would end it by killing Bolan and Dukas.

With that thought locked in his mind Bolan made his decision.

He spent the next few minutes watching, listening, storing tiny details away in case they gave him an advantage when he made the move he was anticipating. He had a plan of sorts.

Granger moved along the cabin, leaning against the fuselage side and studying the package, turning it over in his hands. He took a pocketknife from his pocket and made to slit the packing tape that sealed it.

Dukas was watching Bolan closely. He inclined his head in the direction of the package. She nodded.

Every so often the chopper caught air pockets and currents that flowed back and forth between the mountains. Bolan had observed the armed man assigned to watch them. Each disturbance made him lose concentration for seconds as he braced himself against the unsettling movement of the aircraft. It wasn't much but enough that the muzzle of his weapon would shift off target. Bolan waited, hoping for another bout of turbulence, his body tensed, muscles coiled to push him into instant action.

When it finally came Bolan nearly missed it. The Sikorsky seemed to pause in midair, then dropped a few feet, as the pilot worked the controls. Those few seconds became a moment frozen in time.

Bolan came up off the floor of the chopper and launched himself in the direction of the armed watcher. The guy saw Bolan's move and swung his wavering M-16 back in line. Bolan weaved to the left as he closed on the man, heard the sudden crack of the weapon and felt something burn across his left hip. He slammed into the shooter as the man started up off his seat, his powerful hands closing over the weapon, forcing it upward. Bolan wrenched the assault rifle from the man's grip, then slammed the butt across the side of his head, spinning him away. As the guard went to his knees, Bolan swept the M-16 around, flicking the selector to full-auto and fired off a couple of bursts that had Granger's crew dropping to the floor of the cabin. He directed his fire at the flight cabin, the 5.56 mm slugs smashing into instruments and shattering the Plexiglas canopy.

Movement from the copilot drew Bolan's attention as the man got out of his seat, hauling an automatic pistol from his holster. Bolan hit him with a burst that threw him back against the control console.

A shape moved past Bolan. Dukas reached Granger, who had hunched over to protect himself from the gunfire, and without breaking stride she snatched the package from his hand, turning and running back to where Bolan stood, the M-16 covering Granger's crew.

"Now what?" she whispered.

"I hadn't planned much beyond this," Bolan said.

The chopper swayed suddenly and threw them all to port, the pilot struggling with controls that were threatening to cease working altogether.

"Bastard took out the controls," he screamed. "I'm losing it."

"I don't pay you to fucking lose it," Granger yelled back.

The Sikorsky nosed down, speed increasing with the deadweight of the unstable craft. It swung from side to side, the rugged terrain looming large as they began to lose height with increasing velocity.

"Tell me about this plan again," Dukas said, hanging on to Bolan.

"Later." He took the package from her and zipped it into a pocket of his pants.

"Is there going to be a later?" she asked.

"Hang on."

"Why do I need…"

The helicopter had started to vibrate, the fuselage flexing as the heavy aircraft dropped again, then settled as the pilot managed to regain a degree of control, stabilizing the craft.

Bolan and Dukas were forgotten briefly as Granger and his crew paid attention to what the pilot was doing, mortality seeming the more important consideration at that moment. Edging forward, Bolan positioned himself and Dukas close to the side hatch.

"I see what you mean," she said as the ground became clearer, trees and undergrowth looming larger outside the helicopter. "Aren't we still going too fast?"

"Timber will slow us if we hit," Bolan said.

"Don't you mean *when?*"

The Sikorsky skimmed the tops of trees, shredding the branches. The contact threw the aircraft in a half circle, tilting it. The main rotors sliced through branches, the tail rising suddenly. Throwing the passengers around like corks on the ocean. If Bolan had not been hanging on to a support rail and Dukas holding on to him, they might have been thrown across the cabin. The erratic flight of the chopper increased, the roar of sound as it plowed through the trees was deafening. View ports shattered, the aluminum fuselage ripping open in places. Cold air howled through the rents on the metal. Somewhere electrical cabling crackled as it fused. The front canopy imploded. The pilot was battered before he could vacate his seat, his bloodied body torn and punctured. There was a sudden increase in sound, cracking and splintering that overwhelmed everything else. The chopper seemed to stall in its forward flight then dropped, tearing a destructive path through the trees before it hit the sloping ground below. The impact was less than Bolan might have expected, though there was still force enough to split the fuselage open. Someone screamed as he was catapulted out through the wide gap, the sound shut off as the helicopter rolled over his broken body.

Bolan, hanging on one-handed, yanked the lock bar and freed the side hatch. He was hoping the impact had not pushed the frame out of alignment. He slammed his shoulder against the hatch, freeing it, then worked it along the slides. The moment there was enough of a gap he caught hold of Dukas and launched them out. They hit the slope hard, sliding over the loose surface, ducking their heads to avoid being struck by the falling shale and shattered timber following the helicopter. Bolan raised his head long enough to spot the tangled roots of a tree torn from the earth. The tree itself was wedged against an outcrop. Bolan dug in his heels to slow their descent, then threw out his free hand and caught hold of a twisted root. The sudden wrench jarred his muscles but he refused to let go, and with a sudden jerk they were still. Bolan saw the Sikorsky still sliding down the long slope, trailing smoke and debris in its wake.

The Executioner sat up, ignoring the bruising pain burning the length of his body. He felt something digging into his back and realized it was the M-16. Without conscious thought he had slung the carrying strap over his shoulder and it had stayed with him. He pulled the weapon off his shoulder and checked it out. Apart from being streaked with dirt it appeared undamaged. Bolan checked the magazine, replaced it and cocked the weapon.

Dukas pushed herself to a sitting position, brushing hair back from her battered face. "I used to believe it when they said the great outdoors was good for your health."

Bolan saw the helicopter shudder to a stop some two hundred yards below them. Smoke issued thickly from the engine housing. "Let's go, he said. "We need cover before they start shooting."

Dukas followed his line of sight and saw movement as figures scrambled out of the wrecked chopper. Then the crackle of autofire, slugs raking the slope around Bolan and Dukas. The shooters were firing uphill, and it would take them a few rounds to find their range. Bolan didn't intend to present them with an easy target.

They pushed away from their position, digging in with their feet to gain purchase on the loose slope. Bolan allowed Dukas to move ahead of him so he could check on Granger's men. His close observance paid off when he saw a raised autorifle release a grenade from an M-16 M-203 combo. Bolan slammed into Dukas, driving them both down as the explosive detonated far to their left, sending a mushroom of dirt and snow into the air. Bolan felt the pressure of the blast and the impact of debris against his back.

On his feet, Bolan urged Dukas upright and they angled across the slope, where thick foliage offered temporary cover. As they worked their way in toward the undergrowth, Bolan heard the soft rush of air as another grenade came their way. it struck too far away to do any harm.

Sucking air into their starved lungs, they paused long enough for Bolan to check out the dispersment of Granger's crew. Bolan saw one of them starting up the slope. He seemed to have located an area where the surface of the slope was less treacherous and was making good progress.

"Let's go," he said.

They traveled steadily, aware of the cold that managed to penetrate their weatherproof clothing. Bolan kept an eye on the prevailing conditions, noting that the snowfall showed no signs of stopping. It was made worse by the constant wind that gusted down from the higher slopes, picking up the fallen snow and swirling it about.

The endless spread of the peaks surrounded them. It would have been easy to have given in and allowed defeat to slow them. The constant moving across the rugged terrain didn't appear to be getting them anywhere, but as far as Bolan was concerned they were faced with two distinct and immovable options.

Quit and let Granger take them.

Or keep moving, offering resistance, and make Granger and his crew pay for every foot of ground.

SOMETIME AFTER THEY HAD reached the head of the slope and were trekking through an undulating gully, Bolan reached out to touch Dukas. She turned, a question beginning to form, then saw his signal for silence. Bolan moved close, lowering his voice as he spoke.

"That guy we spotted. I think he's close."

"Are you going to…?"

He nodded.

"I want to keep it quiet in case there are others in the vicinity." Bolan looked around and spotted what he wanted. He indicated a low depression choked with undergrowth. "Cover for you. Now."

Dukas made a wide detour, then angled around to the far side of the depression before dropping flat and sliding under cover. Bolan made a similar move, into some timber, then doubled back and hauled himself onto a jutting outcropping that overlooked the tracks they had made. He crouched on top, leaned over and dropped the M-16 into the snow a few feet away from the outcropping. He would have been the first to admit it was a crude deception and wouldn't fool anyone for long, but his intention was to take advantage of even the briefest opportunity. He had no choice, or time, to do anything else.

The man came around the outcropping, his M-16 raised, muzzle searching. He paused when he spotted Bolan's discarded rifle, making a wide sweep of the area, then reached for the transceiver clipped to his belt.

Bolan came down off the outcropping, slamming into the man's shoulder. The impact took them both to the ground, the rifle spinning from the intruder's hands as he landed. They rolled apart and Bolan recovered fast, gaining his feet. He saw the other man pushing up off the ground, on his knees and reaching for the Beretta holstered on his hip. Closing in, Bolan launched a powerful kick that struck the man's skull, knocking him back, throwing out a hand to steady himself. He raised his head and saw Bolan's follow-up. He tried to avoid it, but Bolan's boot crunched against his left cheek, shattering bone, twisting his head at a deadly angle and slamming him facedown on the ground. Bolan followed down, straddling the prone figure. His neck had been broken.

Bolan rolled the body and helped himself to the combat rig that held extra magazines for the M-16 and the Beretta 92-F. He clipped the rig in place and took the firepower. He freed the transceiver and clipped it to his own belt. He paused to recover his own rifle before he crossed to where Dukas lay concealed.

"We can get out of here now," he said.

She pushed to her feet and joined him, her glance taking in the dead man.

"They're not going to quit, are they?"

"Neither will we," the Executioner said.

He led the way, their travel taking them on a continuing downward route. The snowfall had become a chill drizzle. Farther down the rugged slopes Bolan could see the misty drift of rain where the snow had dispersed completely.

"I think I prefer the snow," Dukas muttered.

They maintained a steady pace, slowed by the treacherous surface of the slopes, where loosened earth and rock made the way difficult to negotiate.

MOVING SHAPES AND SHADOWS warned Bolan that Granger's crew was still on the move. He pulled Dukas into cover as they drew level with a stand of timber. Selecting single-shot Bolan shouldered the M-16, bracing himself against a sturdy trunk as he took aim at the lead figure pursuing them. He stroked the trigger, feeling the rifle buck against his shoulder, and saw the target go down hard. The sound was still drifting across the timbered slopes as return fire began. It was more of a conditioned reflex rather than a deliberate burst, and the slugs were well off Bolan's position.

He motioned for Dukas to move deeper into the timberline, letting the shadows fold around them. They crouched among the dripping foliage, chilled by the sodden clothing they were wearing.

"I'd give anything to be a few days back," Dukas said. "Going back to my nice warm apartment. Sitting with a cup of coffee. Relaxing and..." Her voice faltered. "Damn those people. All I can think of is Tira begging for her life while those bastards cut her to pieces. How could they destroy a young life that way? Another human being."

"They see it as survival. A threat to *their* safety because they see their lives as more important."

"That excuse isn't good enough," Dukas said bitterly.

"I wasn't excusing them. I was telling you how *they* see it."

Bolan raised a hand for silence, gesturing for Dukas to go deeper. He moved the M-16's selector to full-auto, rising so he could check out the sound source that had alerted him. He focused, separating substance from shadow and detailed two armed figures. They were outfitted exactly the same as all the other Granger crew members. He watched them moving in his direction, judging distance, and opened fire, hitting the closest man in the chest. Switching targets, he caught the second guy in the chest and head.

Bolan turned and hauled Dukas upright and took them deeper into the timber as he heard raised voices and the crash of bodies pushing through the foliage. They moved through the heavy growth that grabbed at their clothing and snagged their exposed hands. Underfoot the ground was sodden and spongy. It held them back, allowing their pursuers to stay close.

From overhead, Bolan picked up the beat of a helicopter. It was moving in on their position, and he realized this was why Granger's crew had easily been reinforced. The man and his money could buy however many gunners he needed to back his play and keep the battle in the wilderness where it was undetected.

If Granger wanted a war, the Executioner thought, he could have one.

18

"Dead? All of them?"

Granger absorbed the information. Billingham and Radin. Even Radin's security man, Jatko.

"You want to talk to Billingham's guy?" Marker asked. "He's staying out of sight. The local law is out in force scouring the town, so he has to keep low. Pavlic's dead too, so at least that's taken care of."

"You handle it."

Granger felt a surge of pain from his aching arm and reached up to grip it. He had come out of the downed Sikorsky with little more than the badly bruised arm, but with his pride hurt badly. As soon as Marker had sent the crew out to follow Cooper and the woman, he had used his radio to call in a replacement chopper, with an additional team of shooters. By the time the helicopter had reached them Granger's mood had soured even more. His initial anger had been replaced by frustration and a growing bitterness as he accepted the fact that he had lost the package within a short time of getting his hands on it.

Granger, seated at one of the helicopter's view ports,

glanced at his second in command. "At least we know where we stand, Lee. It comes down to this son of a bitch Cooper. I have to admire him. The way he's come through all this and is still on the move."

"He has to be more than just a federal agent. The way he operates, I'd guess he's got military training backing him, which makes it harder. He knows evasion tactics. Only thing slowing him down is the Dukas woman. If he was on his own, he'd be hitting us even harder," Marker said.

Granger smiled. "Lee, he isn't doing too badly *with* the Dukas woman on his hands."

Marker touched the raw bruises on his face. They extended from his cheek to the hairline and hurt like hell. "I owe that bastard."

One of the chopper's crew approached them.

"I've received an update from the ground team," he said. "They have Cooper and the woman spotted." He showed them a map. "Right about here. Ground visibility is poor. Snow's gone, but it's raining pretty bad. Cooper is moving along this slope. Southwest. In a couple of miles they'll hit a water course. It flows into a deep ravine. If they get in there, it isn't going to be easy to flush them out."

"Can we get to them first?" Marker asked.

"The pilot says yes. The ravine might be tricky for the chopper. Until we hit it we won't know if we can fly through."

Marker nodded. "Tell the pilot to concentrate on getting us to Cooper first. See if we can block off the ravine. Stop them getting inside. Have the men close in and watch for them climbing out. And tell them to watch out for Cooper. He's as slippery as snake oil."

Granger settled back in his seat, reaching for one of the flasks holding hot coffee. "Lee, if we come through this I won't forget it."

"I'll remind you about that," Marker said.

"THERE," DUKAS SAID.

Bolan turned and saw the dark shape of the Sikorsky as it rose above the ridge, driving sheets of rain across the bare rock slope. He felt the draft from the spinning rotors, heard the heavy roar of the turbine as the aircraft swept in at them. He made a grab for Dukas, pulling her off balance so she slid off the wet rock and out of sight.

The barely audible crackle of autofire reached his ears as 5.56 mm slugs danced off the rock surface inches from Bolan. He crouched and angled his own weapon up at the chopper as it swept overhead, releasing a burst of full-auto fire that raked the chopper's underside.

From her position below him Bolan heard Dukas yell. "Damn it, Cooper, get down here. Please."

The Sikorsky curved away, making a wide turn, allowing Bolan an opportunity to reach better cover. He dropped over the lip and slid down the streaming rock to where Dukas crouched. She stared at him, silent for once, her face pale and wet, dark hair plastered against her skull.

Below them the ravine wall fell away in a series of

serrated ledges, widening its span. The rushing water foamed where it hit the rocky sides.

"That chopper can't get below the rim," Bolan said. "Not enough clearance to make it safe."

He reminded himself that restriction wouldn't apply to Granger's armed crew.

The helicopter made its return sweep at that moment, forced to remain above the ravine. It hovered over them like some dark, venomous insect. As Bolan and Dukas worked their way down the uneven wall, someone opened fire. With the slight overhang at the top of the ravine there was little chance of them being hit, but Bolan still registered the snap and whine of the slugs as they struck the rock above them.

They kept moving down the side of the ravine until they were no more than three feet from the swollen mass of water, soaked by the spray that was hurled up at them, and colder than either of them would have ever chosen to be.

The sound of the chopper faded into the background as they moved along the ravine, conscious of the chill water below and choosing hand- and footholds with extreme care. A slip would put them in the freezing water.

The ravine narrowed ahead of them, becoming almost a tunnel formation as the upper walls closed in. Thick foliage and twisted trees formed a dense canopy, shutting out much of the daylight, leaving them in a shadowy near twilight.

Bolan picked out a spot ahead where the lower face

of the ravine extended out to form a level shelf above the rushing water. It offered a safe place for them to rest. Close to the ravine side the shelf escaped even the water spray and was dry. He called to Dukas that they could take a short break, and there was no objection from her. She squatted with her back to the ravine wall, head down.

Bolan listened for the Sikorsky. It was either too far away for him to hear, or perhaps it had landed to put men on the ground. One way or another it was still around. He didn't fool himself into believing Ramsey Granger had backed off.

Down on his heels, Bolan checked his weapon first.

"Matt."

He turned to Dukas. She pushed damp hair back from her face and stared at him.

"I'm cold. Tired. Hungry," she said. "If that makes me a whimpering amateur I don't care. I'm still cold and tired and hungry."

He moved beside her, putting an arm around her shoulders and drawing her close. She was shivering.

"Is this the magic touch to make me feel better?" she asked.

"Is it working?"

"No, frankly, it isn't."

"Well, I'm cold and tired and hungry too."

"Really?" she asked, and when he nodded said, "That doesn't help either, but thanks for the solidarity."

He hugged her close, feeling her rest her head against him. He felt for her condition and wished he could do something to make it better. But until they removed Granger's lingering threat Dukas was going to have to deal with the situation as best she could. Her initial call for help had escalated beyond even Bolan's expectations. The events that had brought them to this isolated corner of Colorado had allowed little time for much else than pure survival. They had been up against a determined enemy and the capricious weather conditions. Bolan figured they were lucky to have reached this far. He drew her closer, his arms enfolding her, using his own body warmth to comfort her as best he could.

Dukas would have stayed exactly where she was, and protested mildly when Bolan told her it was time for them to move on. He helped her to her feet, gently stroking her hair back from her cold face as she stood looking up at him.

"Hey, why don't I wait here? You go on and get help then come back and get me," she said with a weak smile.

"It doesn't work like that. We get out of this together. Okay?" He picked up his weapons and took her arm, guiding her along the ledge. "See where the trees and foliage have overgrown the ravine? We can probably find a spot where we can climb to level ground again."

"Won't Granger have figured that out too? He's probably sitting up there waiting while his men spread out."

Bolan nodded.

"So we shouldn't disappoint him."

THEY MADE THEIR WAY CLOSE to the spot where ravine and vegetation merged, then located themselves behind an outcropping where Bolan was able to observe without being seen. The ravine side had been worn away by constant erosion and water. Behind the outcrop the wall curved in a hollow that formed a semicave. It would at least provide them with some shelter as well as protection. He made Dukas move to the inside corner and made it clear he didn't want her to move until he gave her the word.

He handed her the Beretta and a couple of extra magazines.

Bolan eased to his chosen spot. He was able to see well into the passage. He set the M-16 for single-shot, then settled in to wait. He knew Granger's men would show. They would assess the location and send some of their number into the ravine to scout him out.

After twenty minutes he saw the foliage ripple, the leaves shivering as someone eased into the ravine. A second man followed, three feet to the left of the first man. Bolan leaned forward, focusing on the disturbance. He watched as the descending figures became visible. He maintained his quiet observance as they climbed farther down the ravine.

They were within ten feet of the base of the ravine wall, where a shallow ledge would afford them footholds. The Executioner wasn't about to let them get that far. As the foliage thinned, the men were fully exposed, and Bolan saw his window of opportunity.

He leaned against the outcropping, the M-16 snug

against his shoulder. His finger rested lightly on the trigger as he settled on his first target, the most distant man.

The shot cracked, echoing within the confines of the rock walls. The slug caught the man between the shoulders, pitching him face forward against the rock. He gave a startled cry as he bounced off the rock, desperately scrabbling for a handhold. There was a moment when he seemed to have gained a grip, then he fell back, twisting and hit the swirling water. He was swept out of sight in an instant.

Bolan's second shot came even as the first man was falling. He settled on his target as the man turned, wide-eyed, his mouth opening in a protest against what he knew was going to happen. Bolan's finger stroked the trigger, the rifle made its brittle sound and the target arched back off the ravine wall and followed the first man into the water. All that remained was a blood splash on the pale rock.

A shell casing rang sharply as it hit the rock at Bolan's feet. It spun, rolled and came to rest close to where Dukas crouched. She stared at the bright metal, clutching the Beretta tight against her chest, but said nothing.

Near the top of the ravine Bolan saw more movement. He thought it was yet another incursion but realized it was someone climbing back up the wall. A third man, seeing the fate of his companions, was retreating. Bolan raised the M-16 and viewed the area. The foliage was denser, so it took him a few seconds to identify his target. The man's too eager movements were exposing him. Bolan tracked his target and placed three shots into the area. Cool and precise. He saw foliage shred, picked out the dark-clad shape as the man fell back, hung for a moment, then fell, turning over a couple of times before he struck the ledge at the base of the ravine wall, his body set at odd angles, one leg trapped under his body. Blood seeped from beneath the body and from the back of his skull where it had impacted with the unyielding rock.

Bolan focused on the head of the ravine where the men had started their climb. He laid a half dozen shots into the area to establish his presence, then pulled back from his firing position and slid to a crouch across from Dukas.

"I'm glad I didn't see that," she said, her voice low and shaky. "Will they come again?"

"Depends how much Granger is paying them. They'll need to ask themselves if it's enough to lay themselves on the line any longer. Granger will tell them it's important. In their minds they'll be wondering if *important* is enough to put themselves on the firing line. Three more dead in less than a minute. It's a hell of a price for a wad of cash."

"Where do these men come from?" Dukas asked.

"Ex-military mostly. Men who spent years being trained for just this kind of thing. Then they find the country doesn't need them any longer, so they leave the service with skills no one wants. Some adjust.

Others don't. But there's always someone, somewhere, who needs these men. So they sign on. Money's good. Better than they got in the service. Risk is something they were trained to accept. So they take the money and do the time. Men like Granger use these people to do their dirty work."

A cascade of small stones rattled on the rock face above where they were crouched. Overhead Bolan heard a man curse softly. The rattle of autofire shattered the silence. Slugs hammered at the rock around them, the curve of the ravine wall protecting them. The slugs struck feet away. Shell casings showered down from the shooter's weapon.

"Stay back," Bolan said. He moved along the base of the rock wall, then stepped out and scanned the ravine above him.

Two of them were coming down on ropes, firing wildly now that their presence had been exposed. One of them saw Bolan as he stepped into view. He yelled a warning to his partner and raised his weapon.

The M-16, now set on automatic, crackled harshly, jacking out its shots. The first guy jerked and squirmed on the end of his rope as Bolan's slugs hammered into his body, blowing bloody exit holes. He slumped loosely, then fell.

Swinging the muzzle, Bolan picked up on the second man. The gunner's weapon had already settled on Bolan's position. They fired together. Slugs screamed off the rock face around the man, then cored in as Bolan's aim was adjusted. The man spun on his rope, his throat and head torn open by M-16's repeated bursts.

Bolan was down on one knee, nursing a bloody left side. One of the 9 mm slugs had lodged just under his ribs, above the earlier gash he'd received. He clamped a hand over the wound, feeling blood seeping through his fingers. A wave of nausea rolled over him, and he was forced to stay down until it passed.

Firm hands reached around his shoulders, helping him upright, drawing him back under cover, then eased him down.

"Give me that rifle," Dukas said.

He realized he was still gripping the M-16. She took it and he watched as she removed the spent magazine, took a fresh one from his harness and clicked it into place. She cocked the weapon then propped it against the rock close by. "You're bleeding all over the place."

"Some days you wish you didn't bother to get out of bed," he replied.

"If this was a Western, I'd be tearing strips off my petticoat now to make bandages. See how practical they were in those days?"

"I don't even have a knife to heat so you can dig the bullet out," he replied.

"No whisky?" she asked.

"To sterilize the wound?"

"For me to drink myself into a stupor and forget this nightmare," Dukas said.

Their position was no laughing matter, but her

solemn proclamation hit the spot. Her mouth formed into a smile, and Bolan knew she was a survivor.

Dukas insisted on looking at the wound. The flesh just behind the entry point bulged slightly, and when she gently probed it she could feel the hard outline of the bullet. The wound was bleeding but not profusely.

"It doesn't seem to have gone in too deep. Hasn't severed any blood vessels or it would be bleeding more than it is," Bolan said.

"Is that the good news?"

He shook his head. "No bullet wound has any good news. It needs dealing with, but right now we don't have any way of doing that."

She turned to look away for a moment. Before Bolan could say anything she had made her way to where the fallen man lay. She searched his body, then unclipped the small backpack he wore before scrambling back to Bolan.

"Yes, I know, it was stupid and risky and I should have known better," she muttered.

She opened the backpack and tipped out the contents.

"What have we got?"

She glanced at the contents.

"Folding knife. Throwaway lighter, pack of cigarettes. Hey, small first-aid kit. Oh, I nearly forgot." She reached behind her and produced a water canteen. "It was clipped to his belt."

She opened the canteen and took a swallow. She bared her teeth and sucked in a sharp breath. "That is cold."

She passed the canteen to Bolan. He drank a little.

"I need you to do something for me," he said, picking up the knife and the lighter.

Dukas watched as he opened the knife and examined the cold steel blade. Then he flicked the lighter and held the flame steady, passing the blade of the knife back and forth. When he was satisfied he poured some of the water over the blade to cool it. By this time Dukas was staring at him, eyes wide as she realized what his request was going to be.

"Open that kit and see what's inside," Bolan requested.

"My God, you're serious. You want me to perform one of those *Dr. Quinn, Medicine Woman* operations. Cut you open and take out that bullet?"

"Either that or you might have to carry me out of here on your back."

"You said yourself it isn't a bad wound."

"No," Bolan replied. "I said the bullet hadn't gone in deep. Any bullet wound is potentially bad. The bullet might not kill but infection can. From the bullet itself. Contamination sucked into the wound. Shreds of cloth. Dirt. If infection sets in it spreads. Poisons the body."

"I'm no doctor—"

"Small incision along the length of the bullet. Expose it and get it out." Bolan indicated the first-aid kit. "Let's take a look."

She unzipped the square pack and laid it open.

"Pressure pads, roll of bandage, tape, sealed sterile pads." She gave a nervous laugh. "Couple of pairs of disposable latex gloves."

"Put a pair on now before you touch anything," Bolan said.

Dukas followed his instructions. Despite the queasiness settling in her stomach she realized his argument was sound. There was no alternative. She held up her gloved hands. Bolan handed her the knife.

"When you take the bullet out use the sterile pads to clean the incision. There's going to be blood, so it should help lubricate the wound."

"Matt, this is going to hurt. If my hand shakes—"

"It won't. I trust you," he said.

He lay back, turning slightly so the wound was exposed. Dukas focused on the spot, seeing the discoloration that followed the outline of the bullet. She reached and took a couple of the sterile pads and placed them close by.

"Make the cut just beyond the wound, go the length of the bullet and beyond," he instructed.

"How will I get the bullet out?" she asked.

"Use the blade to probe it. You ready?" he asked.

"No, but I'll do it."

"If I make any noise ignore it. Just keep going once you start."

Kneeling beside him, Dukas used her left hand to stretch the flesh on either side of the discolored bruise. She brought the tip of the knife down, almost touching his flesh, then stopped. She could feel her heart racing. She took a deep breath, steadied her nerves and cut. The knife was incredibly sharp. It sliced through the flesh with ease. She tried to ignore the blood, as she did the involuntary reaction he made. She heard the breath he sucked in. She drew the knife along the hard outline of the bullet. She was surprised at her sudden calm. She felt the tip of the blade slip as it reached the end of the bullet and remembered what Bolan had instructed about extending beyond. Blood was running freely, welling up from the incision and streaming down Bolan's side.

She kept her nerve. The incision lay open as she stretched it with her left hand, fingers warm from the blood. Leaning in closer, she saw the dull gleam of the bullet embedded in the raw flesh. She heard Bolan's harsh breathing. There was no other indication of what he was going through. He was in pain, she knew that, but he was fighting against it.

"I can see the bullet. I'm going to try to get it out," she whispered.

She used the tip of the blade to ease the bullet from the bloody cavity. She went to the tip, where the taper of the metal slug would allow her to ease the knife beneath it. She used her fingers to probe the edges of the incision and force them apart. As she exerted pressure, she heard Bolan give a low groan and for the first time his body arched in protest. She kept probing, felt the flesh give a little and slipped the knife tip beneath the blood-slick bullet. She felt it give and slid the blade a little farther along the underside of the bullet, forcing it up out of the wound until she was able to drop the knife and ease the bullet out with her thumb and finger.

She cast the bullet aside, reaching for one of the sterile packs and tore open the foil covering. Bending over once again, she used the sterile pad to wipe inside the incision, ignoring the fact she was still hurting Bolan. When the pad was sodden with blood she opened a second one and repeated the action, examining the inside of the wound each time she wiped away the fresh blood that still welled up. The wound looked clean—as clean as she was going to be able to judge under the conditions they were in.

Leaning back, she peeled off the gloves and pulled on a fresh pair. Using more of the sterile pads she did her best to stop the bleeding. It took some time before the blood stopped flowing so readily, and she had run out of sterile pads except for one. She wanted to use that beneath the pressure pad when she bandaged it in place.

"You awake?" He had gone very still and quiet. "I need you to sit up in a minute."

He turned his head to look at her. Sweat beaded his pale face.

"You finished?"

"I'm going to put the pressure pad in place and wind the bandage round you. I'll need you to sit up for that. Just take it slow. No way we can sew that incision up, so you'll probably have a scar. On the plus side it isn't too much of an incision so it won't spoil your chances in next year's bikini contest. Well, no more than all your other scars."

"That's taken a weight off my mind," Bolan said.

Dukas dressed the wound. "You're going to need to rest for a while," she said.

Bolan buttoned his shirt and zipped up his thick coat. The clothes felt cold against his body. Like it or not they were going to have to stay put for the moment.

The downside was that Granger's men knew where they were. He had succeeded in taking out a percentage of Granger's crew but at the cost of revealing their position. The unknown was the size of Granger's crew. How many more were waiting above the ravine? And how long would they wait before Granger sent them in?

Bolan pulled the M-16 close, surveying the upper section of the ravine. He could see no movement.

Bolan realized he hadn't given the package much thought since he and Dukas had bailed out of the Sikorsky. He leaned forward and unzipped his pocket, withdrawing the sealed parcel. He sat looking at it.

"Here," Dukas said, passing him the folding knife. "It's time we had a look at that damn thing."

Bolan slit the tape holding the package together. He peeled back the outer layer and exposed a layer of bubble wrap, then beneath that a leather disk holder. He opened the zipper and exposed three shiny disks, each its own plastic sleeve. Bolan read the labels and saw they all referred to business files.

"Which is the disk?" Dukas asked.

"I doubt Pavlic would have labeled it," the soldier stated.

"I guess not. He probably placed it as a hidden file. Maybe even encrypted so it wouldn't show even if someone loaded it. Aaron's the one to access it. He'll know what to do."

"Don't worry about that, honey," someone said. "Our own expert will dig it out."

Three armed figures confronted them, weapons on track. The one who appeared to be in charge stepped forward. He was lean, with pale eyes as cold as the icy water running through the ravine. He was tall, over six feet, and had to bend forward to take the case from Bolan's hand.

His name was Lee Marker.

Dukas glanced at Bolan and saw his slight shake of the head. She could imagine he was thinking the same thing she was. That they had been caught off guard by the stealthy approach of these men, probably during the time she had been removing the bullet from Bolan's side. It was a mistake that had cost them dearly.

"You know, I should be really upset with you two," Marker said. "Hell of a chase you led us on. And look how many of my boys you took out. Mr. Granger has been put to a great deal of trouble."

"I'm all broken up hearing that," Bolan said.

Marker smiled easily. He glanced across at Dukas.

"Nothing to say this time, Erika? No? There'll be time for that later. On your feet. Let's get out of here."

"He's hurt," Dukas said. "He can't just—"

One of the armed men laughed.

"You hear that, Lee? Aw, he's hurt. Maybe we should send for a rescue chopper."

"And maybe I should off this bastard right here and now," Marker said, his light mood vanishing in an instant.

He stood over Bolan, the muzzle of his M-16 lining up with Bolan's head.

"Please, no," Dukas screamed, her voice high and shrill.

The terror in her words drew attention. Even Marker shunted his gaze to her for a split second.

And knowing he had been offered a chance by the outburst, the Executioner took it.

19

Bolan knew his wound was bleeding again. The tearing burn registered as he snatched up the M-16 that lay partly concealed at his side. He turned the muzzle in Marker's direction. He ignored the pain because if he didn't he was going to be dead anyway.

Reactions were often dictated by the mood of the moment. With Bolan under his gun, Marker was feeling good. The woman's plea only added to his enjoyment of the moment, and like many who thrived on the strength of gaining power over others, he glanced her way to savor the fear in her face.

But when saw her face—the gleam of triumph in her bright eyes—he knew he'd been tricked. There was no fear. No terror. Only a mocking expression.

Marker brought his attention back to Bolan and realized he had committed a lethal mistake.

The heel of Bolan's boot slammed hard against Marker's left knee, the impact knocking him off balance. Bolan rolled to a crouch, his finger stroking the M-16's trigger repeatedly. His bursts hit Marker's backup team, kicking them off their feet. They sprawled across the shelf of rock, bodies squirming under the impact of Bolan's shots. He put final head bursts into them, ensuring there would be no comeback.

Bolan met Marker as the man recovered his balance and hauled his own weapon back into play. There was no hesitation as Bolan swung the M-16 around in a savage arc that clouted Marker across the side of his skull. The blow dropped him to his knees, leaving him gasping in pain. Bolan hit him a second time, driving him facedown on the rock, blood pouring from the gash in his head. The soldier bent forward and retrieved the disks.

The Executioner stepped back, clenching his teeth against the surge of pain from his side. He leaned against the rock face as Dukas moved to his side, concern in her eyes.

"That wasn't the best idea you've ever had," she said.

Bolan looked beyond her to the sprawled bodies, then down at Marker's prone figure.

"Your performance worked," he said. "We got a result. Go clear their weapons."

She moved to the bodies, bringing back the guns they had been carrying. Then she did the same with Marker.

"Check his backpack," Bolan said.

Marker carried extra ammunition, a powerful transceiver and a bundle of plastic restraints.

"He brought them for us," Dukas said.

She knelt beside Marker and pulled his hands behind his back, using one of the plastic restraints to bind his wrists and not being gentle in the process.

Bolan had slid down the rock to a sitting position, holding one hand to his bleeding side. Sweat beaded his unshaven face.

"Now what?" Dukas asked.

"I'm considering our options."

Bolan examined the transceiver in his hand. It was a state-of-the-art model, with a digital readout. He switched it on and heard someone speaking.

"Lee...I heard shooting...talk to me..."

Bolan keyed the transmit button.

"He's tied up at the moment. That you, Granger?"

"Who is this? What are... *Cooper?* Is that you, Cooper?"

"You must be running out of options, Granger. And men. Even with your clout you can't snap your fingers and make them appear."

"Cross me, Cooper, and I'll make you pay."

"Tone it down, Granger. Threats don't impress me. Or intimidate. Big man on the Washington circuit? When we see exactly what you were involved in you'll be closing up shop."

"I don't think so. I'm too important. Contract work I do for the military isn't going to be stopped because of something that happened more than ten years ago. You'd be surprised what is overlooked in the cause of national security. I'll be protected. I'll buy my way out," Granger shouted.

"Understand, Granger. It isn't the military you have to account to. It's me. And I don't plea bargain. Or compromise," the Executioner replied.

The pause was enough. Granger was considering Bolan's words. He was unsure who he was dealing with, but disturbed by the chilling words he had just heard.

"Go to hell, Cooper…"

Bolan heard the unit click as Granger switched off.

"Sounds as if you touched a nerve there," Dukas said.

"He still thinks he can worm his way out of this. Now that all his partners are dead he only has to save himself."

Bolan slowly pushed to his feet and stepped out from the overhang. He stood upright, feeling the chill rain on his upturned face. The sound of engines powering up told him exactly what he had expected. It was Granger's helicopter lifting off. The man was leaving, abandoning his people and making his escape.

Bolan glanced back and saw Lee Marker raising his bloody head. The expression on Marker's face told Bolan he had heard the sound too.

"Loyalty's such an endearing quality in a person," Bolan said.

BOLAN SAT WITH HIS BACK TO the rock as Dukas made an attempt to repair the damage he'd done to his bandaged side. He was scrolling through the frequency band on the transceiver in an attempt to make contact with someone, anyone, though he knew it was a near-futile exercise because of presettings.

The voice coming through made Dukas look up.

"…Striker…respond…Striker…"

The unmistakable voice of Jack Grimaldi.

"J.G., this is Striker. Talk to me. Where are you?"

"Striker, stay on air so I can get a fix on your position. Christ, Sarge, your voice never sounded so good. You guys okay?"

"Both of us. A little shop-soiled, but we're good."

Grimaldi broke off for a moment. "Okay, I got you on-screen. Five minutes from your location."

"Any joy on Casper?"

"Sorry, Sarge. I couldn't locate him. I've been sweeping the area. Bodies, sure. Even a couple of downed choppers but no Bud."

"He was a good friend."

"The way things have been going, Sarge, I'm glad I found you two. Hey, Bud would have gone down fighting. It was the way he was."

Bolan spoke to Grimaldi over the transceiver until the Stony Man pilot hovered over the ravine, lowering a winch cable and harness. Dukas went up first. When the cable returned Bolan strapped it to Marker and waited for its return before he was hauled out of the ravine. The moment he was inside, Grimaldi retracted the winch and closed the hatch. The pilot eased the chopper away from the ravine and put it down on solid ground. He joined Bolan.

He had been expecting Bolan and Dukas to be in rough shape. When he saw them, he tipped his cap to the back of his head and gave a sigh.

"What in hell have you guys been up to? Looks like you crawled over the Rockies on your hands and knees."

"What's a girl to do?" Dukas said. "Not a beauty salon open between here and D.C."

She had dropped onto one of the side seats, clutching her arms around her body as she tried to get warm. With the secession of activity over, her body was starting to react to the hardship and exposure it had been through.

Grimaldi, sensing her condition, moved into action. He opened lockers and produced blankets and thick coveralls.

"You need to get out of those wet clothes," he said. "You too, Sarge. Where to?" Grimaldi added.

"Maple Lake. We can leave him there." He turned to indicate the silent Lee Marker. The man had slumped down on one of the side seats, staring out through the side port.

"Never mind him," Dukas said. "We need to get Cooper, here, to a doctor."

Grimaldi had seen the bloody patch on Bolan's side. He hadn't missed the other severe bruises and cuts both of them were exhibiting.

"And did you get your package?" he asked.

Bolan reached into the pocket of his discarded coat and brought out the disk holder.

"He got it," Dukas said.

Bolan reached across and took her hand.

"We got it."

Maple Lake, Colorado

BOLAN HAD ESTABLISHED A computer link with Stony Man. "Were you able to read the files I sent," he asked.

"Took awhile," Kurtzman said over the voice link.

"Pavlic had the film buried in an encrypted file. But we opened it up. It's as good as an indictment as you'll ever see." He hesitated. "You want to see it?"

"Go ahead," Bolan said.

He felt the Maple Lake police force had a right to see what was behind the trouble that had descended on their community.

Bolan felt Dukas rest her hand on his shoulder as the screen filled to show the segment. Behind Bolan and Dukas the Maple Lake law force stood and watched the scene as the six prisoners were led from a parked truck to stand on the edge of a rain-sodden pit. Behind them stood an armed trio and off to the side more figures watched. There was a brief exchange of words. The female of the six prisoners had a heated outburst before the abrupt and final act as the armed men opened fire, from no more than a few feet. The six victims toppled into the pit. There was an added surreal quality there being no sound, like some old silent newsreel. Only these digital images were in color, the images sharp and detailed. Detailed so that the perpe-trators of the massacre were fully identified as the cameraman focused on each one in turn so that there was no mistaking any of them. Ten years back they had been thinner, with more hair, but there was no denying who they were. Bolan noticed that through the entire sequence Pavlic kept his gaze averted and would not look at either the victims or in the direction of the cameraman he knew was there. His filmed record, rather than protecting him, had in fact been the catalyst that brought about the deaths of those involved.

Full circle.

After the scene faded there was an uncomfortable silence in the office. Sheriff Garrett sat slumped in a chair and shook his head at what he had seen.

"We are a sad excuse for a species sometimes," he said. "Poor bastards there slaughtered so a bunch of dirtbags could line their pockets."

"All of us here were affected by them," Dukas said.

"I'd say there's a whole mess that's going to need cleaning up when all this comes out," Garrett said.

Bolan nodded. "Once all the names are verified and past and current deals brought into the open."

"They're starting to come through now," Kurtzman said over the link. "Since we spoke to Sarajevo and downloaded a copy of the film they've already identi-fied a number of people. The findings agree with what we'd already pieced together. Including the victims. One of them, the woman, was an undercover operative already digging into the group's activities. Sarajevo police are looking to arrest the one remaining guy who stayed behind to mind the store, Sev Malik. There is another one, in a coma after an accident. He might have been hit by his own friends. Maybe some fallout within the group. Colorado State Police were called to an airstrip following the discovery of a body. They were on alert to information we put out through Justice. When they checked ID the guy turned out to be Karel Medusku. Double tap to the back of the head. Federal agents are dropping in on Granger Industries as we speak. He won't be able to buy his way out of this."

"Okay," Bolan said. "We'll be back ASAP once we get checked out. I'll bring the disk with me. Thanks."

He cut the connection.

"Hell of a day," Sheriff Garrett muttered into his coffee mug.

BOLAN WATCHED DUKAS AS SHE moved to a quiet corner of the office. She slumped in a chair, hugging a thick parka around her body, staring down at the floor. He crossed to join her, crouching beside the chair.

"Hey, you shouldn't frown like that, young lady."

She looked at him, smiling wearily.

"No."

She leaned forward and touched his face, kissing him gently. Bolan saw the tears in her bright eyes.

"That was from the two of us," she said. "From me *and* Tira."

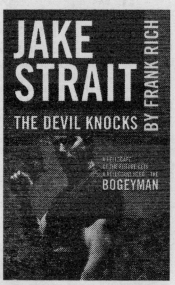

James Axler
Outlanders

SKULL THRONE

RADIANT EVIL

Buried deep in the Mayan jungle amidst a civilization of lost survivors and emissaries of the dead, lies a relic that hides secrets to the prize— planet Earth. In sinister hands, it guarantees complete and absolute power. Kane and the rebels have just one chance to stop a rogue overlord from seizing glory, but must face an old enemy to stop him.

Available May 2007, wherever you buy books.